Silver

His Protectors

Book 2

By

Ronna M. Bacon

Deuteronomy 31:6 Be strong and of a good courage, fear not, nor be afraid of them: for the LORD your God, he it is that does go with you; he will not fail you, nor forsake you.

Psalms 91:4 He shall cover thee with his feathers, and under his wings shalt thou trust: his truth shall be thy shield and buckler.

NKJV

Table of Contents

The early morning sun filtered through the leaves in the forest. It was early summer and the daily heat was already starting to form. Silver Sloane walked slowly along one of the paths in the quarry near her home. It had totally reforested itself after the quarry had ceased its operation. The sounds of nature awakening and then others seeking their sleep hit her ears. She sighed. She was bored and felt uncomfortable. Something was about to happen to her. Silver just prayed that it wasn't what had happened to her friend and team mate, Timothy. He did have an adventure but had found his life mate, Tate, through it all. All the members on Richard's security team were close and this had now changed the dynamics. Sloane wished for someone for herself, the knight that her mother had woven into her stories as a child.

Sloane tugged her ball cap down further over her black curly hair that she had pulled back into a low pony tail. Her curiously-coloured gray eyes seemed to reflect the angry waves of a lake. Her footsteps slowed for a moment as she turned her head to listen. She had heard something, not sure what it was. Her steps picked up their speed as she broke into a low run, something that she enjoyed. Only, today, she wasn't prepared to have to slide to a stop, her hands rising as she saw the man in front of her.

The man simply stood and watched her, his eyes not moving from her. She couldn't get around him and had no desire to turn her back on him. She watched carefully, assessing the situation and not liking what she could see.

"Excuse me? Can I pass?" Silver's voice was low although it sounded loud in her ears. She winced at that.

The man refused to speak, his eyes lifting for a moment to look behind her. Silver sensed someone approaching behind her. She jumped as she felt arms around her, not to entrap her. Instead, she felt safe. That bothered her as well. She didn't date, didn't have a male in her life other than her father and her brother. So, who was this?

Sorley McTavish had been out for his own run, the quarry a favourite place for him to escape to. He had been driven that morning to go there, God simply telling him that he had to and that he was needed there. He had watched the young lady running ahead of him until she had disappeared around a bend in the path. His steps had slowed and stopped as he watched the confrontation, if that's what it could be called, ahead of him. Sorley had walked forward, not sure if she was safe and then simply encircled her with his arms. Silver had jumped at his touch and then relaxed back again him. He didn't think this was normal for her as he had watched her around town and around their church.

"I missed you in the parking lot, sweetheart. I didn't think that you were here already." Sorley's baritone voice soothed the fear that was rising within Silver.

"Did you?" Silver played along with him, her eyes not moving from the man ahead of her. She frowned. *No, I don't know him. I feel like I should know him. He means me harm, that much I do know. Only, who is this behind me? I trust him without knowing who he is. That's also unusual for me.*

Sorley's steps took them backwards, Silver moving with him. His deep green eyes searched the area. The sun reflected off the auburn hair that he kept slightly longer than was currently the style. They backed away around the bend before Sorley reached for Silver's hands and then pulled her with him back towards the parking lot.

Silver ran with him, her hand tight in his. She heard running footsteps behind them and picked up her speed. Sorley pulled her to a stop and then onto a nearby animal path, carefully pulling the brush back behind them. He reached to hug Silver, finding her hugging him back. They listened as they heard running footsteps and then stared at one another.

"Are you okay?" Sorley's voice was low as he searched the area around them. He needed to get Silver back to her car.

"I am. Thank you. I'm sorry. I don't think that we have met." Silver's eyes were puzzled. She trusted him and that was something she just didn't do either. She didn't trust someone this quickly.

"I'm Sorley McTavish. I've seen you around town and around church." He grinned for a moment.

Silver studied him and then nodded.

—

"I'm Silver Sloane. You've been here for a couple of years." She turned as she heard more footsteps that meant the man had returned and this time he was not alone.

Sorley nodded, glancing around and then tugging her with him along the path. The undergrowth brushed at them, Sorley going before Silver and holding the larger branches back from the path for her.

They stopped abruptly near the parking lot. There was a lot more traffic there than either one of them had found. In fact, their cars had been the only ones in the parking lot when they started out. Now, there were a number of vehicles and men pacing around.

Silver sighed. There was no way that they could leave. Her phone was out as she sent off a text to Richard. He not likely would get it for a while as he had early morning meetings that he needed to be at. The other three on her team, Timothy, Stephen, and Naomi, were away for the day, off on their own time.

Sorley studied her and then the parking lot. He needed to get Silver away. He could feel danger approaching her and didn't know how to protect her. His work as a financial investigator didn't allow him to protect ladies in real life. All he knew was that he wanted to do that.

"Silver? What now?" Sorley's voice was low.

"I don't know. Those men are not here for our health." Silver kept searching for a way out. She pointed off to the side. "That way. There's a path that we can follow. I've sent a text to my boss but he won't be able to respond for a while. He's in a meeting."

"Okay. So, we're on our own." Sorley followed her, their feet set down carefully to minimize the noise. His arms came around Silver as she stopped short. "Silver?"

Silver didn't speak, just kept her eyes on the gun held on her. She sighed. *This worked out so well, didn't it? And now what, Lord? We're not getting out of this right away?*

Sorley and Silver were forced to walk towards the centre of the quarry, Silver's hand once more in Sorley's. They watched as the men paced around them as if they were waiting for someone else to appear or for orders to come through.

The first man simply stood and watched them before he approached them. Silver's scream broke through the silence as the man's weapon rose and fell, the butt of the gun hitting hard on Sorley's head, dropping him to the ground. Silver spun, ready to defend herself before her hands were grabbed roughing and tied behind her. She was shoved forward once more, hearing the noise of Sorley pulled to his feet and then draped over one of the men's shoulder.

Pushed past where she would normally have turned back, Silver's heart was heavy. They were in danger and could not escape. How did they get away? She couldn't run and leave Sorley. That was a given, she knew, but there was no way he would be able to escape.

Deep in the forest, Silver was pulled to a stop and then pushed down on the ground. She gave a small whimper as she landed hard on a rock, the roughness biting into her calf. She too was bound hand and foot. Sorley's body was dropped hard beside her, his feet now bound. The men stood and watched them before they turned and walked away.

Not one word had been said. Silver shuffled around until she was able to sit, her eyes on the trail before dropping to Sorley. *God? I know that You are there. I just wish this was different. I just don't know how we'll get out of this.*

—

Chapter 2

Hours seemed to have passed but afterwards, Silver was never sure just how long it had been. She wiped at the sweat on her face, brushing it away with the shoulder of her T-shirt. Her eyes were constantly moving between searching for a way out and then on Sorley. She frowned as she remembered how that she had reacted when he had approached her. Once more she tried to take in the fact that she had let him hug her and then hold her hand. That was not her. It had to have been God, she thought. How else would that have happened? But it still didn't explain what was happening.

Silver grew thirsty and then went past that moment, swallowing hard to try and keep her throat and mouth lubricated with saliva. She inched closer to Sorley, a frown once more on her face. He had not moved, had not roused. She was deeply worried. *God, are You here? You tell me that You are. Please, Lord, we need help. Only no one can find us. Only You know where we are.*

A soft rustling in the bushes failed to raise Silver's head. She had dozed off, too tired to keep awake. She had shifted to a prone position, her head pillowed on Sorley's arm. She had tried to rouse him. Only that had not worked. He simply didn't rouse.

The man who appeared from the bushes stopped abruptly, his eyes on Silver and then Sorley. *There shouldn't be anyone else here,* he thought. He was always here on his own. So where did these two come from? He approached carefully, his feet in the worn, broken shoes set carefully onto the path. He stood, eyes watchful before he reached to touch Silver's hair and then reached to feel for a pulse. She was alive, he was relieved to find out before he reached to assess whether Sorley was alive. He stood upright again, a scowl on his face. These were intruders and intruders needed to be punished.

The man stooped once more, drawing Sorley to his feet and then over his shoulder. He disappears into the brush and was gone for a while before he returned. He stood, head moving as he looked for signs of any other intruders. Silver was gathered into his arms and he strode away, heading for his ramshackle abode.

Sorley roused briefly as he heard the man returning before he was lost again into the darkness that seemed far too black. The man studied him and then Silver before she was laid on the rough broken wooden floor near the makeshift fireplace. He would not help them out, he decided, even though he had cut the bonds tying them motionless.

Silver shifted on the floor, uncomfortable but not knowing why. She raised her head once more, her vision blurry as she stared around. Her hand went up to move her hair from her face, frowning that it was loose. Silver was certain that she had put it into a pony tail. She was just too out of it to realize that it still was. She glanced towards the body laying beside her before she shifted over enough to touch him. Sorley did not move and she didn't understand why. Silver's head was back on the floor as she tried to figure out what was going on and just who this man was with her.

Late that night, Sorley fought his way back up from the darkness, just to find dimness in front of his eyes. He shifted his position, glancing around. *He didn't know this place,* he thought. *Where was he?* Feeling something on his shoulder, he stared at the lady laying there, her hand tight on his. He didn't know her, he didn't think but he couldn't think as his head hurt too much. His gaze shifted as he stared around the room, not recognizing it. Sorley sighed. *What had he gotten himself into? And just where was he and just who was this with him?*

The man who had rescued them watched from across the room, a battered tin cup held in his crooked fingers. Life had not been good to him and it showed. He banged the cup down and stalked across the room, to stare down at them. He cackled in glee for a moment. *Yes,* he thought, *he could and would put them to work in his grow-up operation. They were just who he needed to expand his plot.* He didn't care that they were persons with families and friends. They had been dropped into his world and they would never leave. He just needed them to wake up. He reached to tug at the shackles that he had crafted and placed on their ankles. They would not be going anywhere, he was certain of that.

The early morning light that filtered through dirty windows roused Silver. She rubbed at her face before she sat up. Her mind was clearer. She stared around, not recognizing at all where she was. She shifted her sitting position, a hand resting on Sorley's chest before she stared at him.

—

"Sorley? Can you wake up?" Her voice was low and she had to clear her throat a number of times in order to speak. She shook him, finding no response. *This is not good,* she thought. *I need to get him to help but I don't know where I am.* She reached for her phone, finding that she had no cell service. *This is just great. God, where are You? We need help. Only it doesn't look as if I'll find it.*

She rose, not hearing the clanking of the metal shackles and tried to walk forward. The shackles stopped her from taking a full step and she fell, landing hard on her hands and knees. She stayed in that position, the jarring of hitting the floor driving the breath from her. She shifted to sit, frowning at her ankles before she reached to touch the metal. Silver had no idea who had done this but she was afraid. More afraid that she had ever been. Given that she worked on a security team that protected people, Silver knew how to defend herself. She just hadn't been given that opportunity to do so.

She sighed, the sigh seeming to come from her very toes. Silver had no idea what was going on or who had done this. She just prayed that she could get away, get Sorley away and then find some way to get them home. Only, she had no idea where they were exactly

Silver moved closer to Sorley as she saw him trying to rouse, his eyes opening and closing and his head tossing and turning. Her hand rested on his shoulder, stopping the movement for a moment. Sorley's eyes stayed open at last, a frown on his face. Silver could see the pain in his eyes and in the lines on his face. *He must have a horrible headache,* she thought. *I don't have anything to help him. And I don't know how we'll get away. Someone has taken us captive and shackled us. I just wish I knew why. God, I know that You are here, that You have promised to be here and protect us. I just don't understand.*

Sorley's voice cut through her thoughts.

"Where are we?" He had tired to raise himself up to a sitting position but had found that impossible to do. His head was pounding, and he didn't understand why.

"I don't know, Sorley. I wish I did." Silver stood once more, careful in how she moved, searching for a way out but not finding one. "We're trapped for now." When he didn't respond, she sighed and turned back to him. He had drifted off again, something that she was expecting to happen over and over.

—

Chapter 3

Richard stood outside Silver's home, worried about his team mate and friend. He rang the bell again before he stepped back to the edge of the front porch. She should have been home, he knew. It was a Saturday and she always did her chores on that day. He was worried. Naomi had approached him earlier that day, simply stating that Silver had not shown up for lunch as they had planned on. Richard looked at her, grabbed at her arm, and pulled her towards his truck. Now, he stood on her porch as Naomi searched around the house.

"Richard? I don't see that she's been here for a while." Naomi was worried about her friend and team mate. "This is not like her." With the house key in her hand, she approached the door. "Her car's not here."

"This is out of character for her. She's good about letting us know if she's delayed in meeting one of us. Let's look through her house. I hate to do this, but I don't know that we have much of a choice." Richard followed Naomi into the house, the coolness of it a welcome relief from the heat of the day. "You're more familiar with her home."

"I am. Let's look through it. If she's not here and there's no sign of her, I think we'll need call in the guys and then Bill."

"I agree. Bill is on call this weekend, he told me. There are too many criminal investigations on the go for our friend, the detective." Richard gave a quick grin before he walked down the stairs to the basement, hearing Naomi's quick steps walking through the house. They met at the back door, both puzzled at not finding her.

"This is not right, Richard. Where is she? I know that she was planning on a run or walk early this morning. She didn't tell me where though." Naomi chewed at her bottom lip, her eyes on the bright flowers that lined the fence all the way around the backyard.

"She didn't? That's not like her."

"No, it's not. She's been troubled for a bit. I talked to her brother last night. She's not talking to her family."

"And she's not talking to us." Richard's phone was out as he sent off a quick text to the other two members of their team, Timothy and Stephen. "I can't remember if Timothy and Tate were in town today or if they had taken off."

"They're around. I spoke with Tate earlier. She's trying hard to stay strong in spite of what they went through. She just needed to vent about her parents."

"And she does. I still don't understand how they did what they did." Richard turned away as he dialled Bill's number. "Bill? How busy are you?" Richard grinned at the grumble that Bill gave. "Listen. We're at Silver's place. We can't find her. She didn't turn up for lunch with Naomi."

"She didn't?" Bill Buckley, chief detective for the Elmton police force, sighed. Another one, he thought. "When did you last see or speak with her?"

"For myself, it was as we left last night, around four I think it was. Naomi said they spoke around eight. I don't know if she spoke to the guys or not."

"I'm on my way. You're at her place?" Bill shut his car door, staring through the windshield at the crime scene he had just left.

"We are. Naomi said that Silver had planned a long walk or run this morning. She didn't say where thought."

"There are a lot of places to do just that." Bill pulled away from the house where the triple murder had happened. He was burning out once more, he thought. "Let me know if she shows up. I'll put out a bulletin on her. I don't like this, Richard, not after what happened with Timothy."

"I know. We'll be here." Richard tucked his phone away. *He wasn't happy at all,* he thought. *Where is she, Lord? And how do we find her?*

Timothy and Stephen walked slowly towards Richard and Naomi. Timothy's lady, Tate, had insisted that she had to be there. She just wasn't sure what she could do to help.

"Richard? Any sign of her?" Timothy's hand was tight on Tate's, his eyes searching the ones waiting for them.

"Not a one. We've been through the house, searched the yard, and are now waiting for Bill to show up." Richard paced, his hands clenching and unclenching. All of his team mates were special to him, dear friends to them all. He didn't want to see anything happen to any of them.

Stephen walked away from them, walking across the street where he could see one of her neighbours waiting. He spoke to the man for a bit before he headed back towards his friends.

"Stephen?" Naomi waited, knowing that Stephen was troubled.

"He hasn't seen her. He was up early, around seven he said, and her car was gone by then." Stephen spun in a circle. "There is someone watching us."

"There always is." Richard walked towards Bill as he parked. "Bill?"

"Any sign of her, Richard?" Bill had hoped and prayed that by this time, Silver would have shown up.

Richard's head was shaking as he rubbed as his cheek.

"Not a one. I don't like this, Bill. She is always good at keeping us aware of what is going on. And her family has not heard from them. She was supposed to meet her brother for coffee and didn't. He didn't think too much of it. She sometimes does this."

Bill nodded, walking through the house himself. He didn't see anything overt that was out of place. Naomi would have told him if there had been.

"Okay. So where is she? Where does she like to go and run? Other than the obvious place?" Bill turned to the others. He was at a loss to know where to search.

"She usually runs or walks in town." Naomi drew a deep breath. "I don't like this, Bill."

"None of us do." Bill's eyes were on Tate. "Tate?"

Tate hesitated to speak, being a relatively new friend to the group.

"I talked to her last night, just talking about whatever. She said something about running at a quarry. She does that on occasion, just when she wants solitude."

Bill stared at her, his hand on his phone.

"A quarry? She said that?" At Tate's nod, he walked away from them, his phone out. "Andrew? That quarry outside of town? It's used for walking and running, correct?"

"It is." Andrew McBeth, the town police chief, stood in his kitchen, his little girl in his arms. "Why?"

"Silver's disappeared. She told Tate that she was thinking of running in the quarry today."

Andrew drew in a breath, his eyes on his wife, Phoebe.

"That's a big place to search, Bill, and we're at night now. It's hard to search, too. It's so overgrown."

"I know, Andrew. I suggest that we call in Tad's wife and her dog. But that would have to be tomorrow."

"That won't work. They're away on vacation for the next two weeks." Andrew's hand rubbed at his daughter's back, soothing her. "Do what you can. We'll talk in the morning."

Chapter 4

The next morning, the group had gathered at Richard's home, mingling around the kitchen. He watched them, worrying about them all but more worried about Silver. This was out of character for her, he knew.

"Richard?" Naomi stopped in front of him, her eyes searching his face. "There has been no word."

"No word at all. Bill had an officer drive out to the quarry. There were no vehicles there. If she was there, then she's left. And who knows where she is?"

"Or else she's still there, and someone has taken her car." Timothy knew what he was stating. He just didn't have to like it.

"That's true as well, Timothy." Stephen sipped at his coffee before he set the mug aside. "I talked to her brother this morning. He hasn't heard from her. He did mention that she seemed worried about something. When he asked her, she just shook her head and told him not to worry. As if that would ever happen. Seamus will never stop worrying about his sister."

"No, he won't." Richard reached for the maps that he had printed off the night before. "This is the quarry. Bill is right. It will be difficult to search. It is very overgrown. The only real path runs through the centre of it and loops back. It's hard to see if there are any other paths."

"I was out there a couple of months ago." Timothy took the map, holding it for Tate to look at. "You're right. There are some game trails, many in fact, but the only trail that anyone could walk comfortably would be that one. Or else walk the top perimeter." He paled at a thought, Tate's arm coming around him.

Stephen had been watching him.

"I don't like what you're thinking, Timothy."

"I don't either. Let's pray, people, and then make some plans." Richard led them off in prayer, pausing as he finished. *God, please protect our friend. Bring her home safe and sound. We don't want to see her hurt or have her lost to us forever.*

Tate frowned as she studied the map. There was something niggling at her mind, something that Silver had said. She just couldn't bring it to mind at the moment.

"Tate?" Richard waited patiently, knowing that Tate would speak when she was ready.

"Richard? There is something about that quarry that Silver mentioned. I just can't remember it."

"That's okay. You'll remember when you can."

"I know. I just don't know if it's important or not." Tate walked away, Timothy walking after her.

"Tate?" Timothy hugged her, knowing that she was upset. Silver had become a good friend to her and that was a fact he was glad about.

"Timothy? Where is she? I don't like this." Tate glared at him as he laughed.

"I know that you don't. None of us do. Come on, my love. We're heading out that way. We'll walk through the quarry and see what we can discover."

Three hours later, the group met once more at the entrance to the quarry. They had walked the paths. The men had taken time to try and walk through some of the animal paths but had not made it very far.

Andrew watched as they walked back towards him. He had been contacted by someone from the street, an undercover officer, who had simply stated that there were rumours of a grow up operation in the quarry. He hadn't any more information than that rumour. Andrew beckoned Bill to one side.

"No sign of her, Bill?"

Bill shook his head.

"It's like she was never on earth. There's just no way to find her in here. I wish we could call in a search and rescue group."

"Try Bradon from the Barnabas Foundation. His dog is trained in search and rescue." Andrew had already put in a call to Barnabas Carey, the one who was in charge of the Foundation at that point. He was just waiting for a call back.

"I will." Bill watched his friends, seeing the defeat in their stance. "This is hard on them, Andrew. After what Tate and Timothy went through, we were praying that no one else of them would face danger."

"We do that, Bill, but it's in God's hands. He has allowed this. I don't know why." Andrew waited as Richard approached. "Richard?"

"Thanks for coming, Andrew. You're taking time from lunch with your family."

Andrew shrugged. He had dropped off Phoebe and their little one at his parents'. They had simply prayed for Silver and then sent him on his way.

Bill walked back towards him.

"We have a problem, Andrew. There is someone else missing. Sorley McTavish is missing. He hasn't been seen since Friday either."

Andrew stared at him before sharing a look with Richard. *We're at it again,* he thought. *Another couple missing and in danger. How do we do this, Lord?*

"Sorley? I wasn't aware that Sorley and Silver knew each other."

"They may through church. This complicates it." Bill was away, heading for his vehicle. He needed to speak with Sorley's family and then head for his home. This was not how today was to have gone.

Andrew watched him walk away before he turned to Richard.

"Richard?"

Richard shrugged, not sure what to say.

"I don't know, Andrew. I really don't know. We need to search here to rule out that they aren't here, but there are other areas to search." He looked around.

"Unfortunately, we don't have any security cameras to show that either one of them was here."

"No, we don't." Andrew paused. "We can ask the occupants of the houses along the road. I have someone working on that. There may be security cameras that would show them."

Richard nodded, his eyes on his three team members. This was not what they needed. After what Timothy and Tate went through, they had prayed that no one else did.

Chapter 5

Richard walked back towards his house. It had been three days since they discovered Silver was missing and then finding out that Sorley was well. They had tried to search the quarry but it just hadn't happened. That had frustrated them.

Stephen looked up from where he had seated himself on the front steps. He had been back through the quarry after they had finished work and still had not found any evidence of either one.

"Richard? Any word?"

Richard shook his head, sitting beside Stephen. He leaned forward, his elbows resting on his knees. He listened to the sounds around him.

"Not a word. And I was praying that you would have found them."

"I tried, Richard. I really tried. There just isn't any way to find them. I spoke with Bradon just before you appeared. He's going to head this way tomorrow with Kade, his dog, just to see what they can find out. Andrew hasn't been back in touch either.

"No, he hasn't. That doesn't surprise me." Richard sighed, raising his eyes as he watched a car coming towards them. "I don't recognize that vehicle."

Stephen peered at it, not sure either who it was. They both watched as it came to a stop and a tall older man stepped out and then approached them.

"Can I help you?" Richard was on his feet, a frown on his face before it cleared. "You're Shannon McTavish?"

"I am. Sorley's father. And you are Richard?" He looked past Richard to where Stephen was on his feet. "And Stephen?"

"That's correct. How can we help you?" Richard pointed towards his house. "Come on in. We were just about to find some food. You're welcome to join us."

"That's not necessary." Shannon was hesitant to enter Richard's home, not sure if he should even have come.

"At least have some coffee with us." Richard reached to flick on the coffee pot even as Stephen reached for the meal that was in the crockpot. Richard had a habit of setting a meal in the morning to be ready for him when he got home.

"That would be good. Thank you." Shannon sat, not sure what he expected to hear. He accepted at last the plate of food set in front of him.

Richard set aside his plate as he finished his meal, his eyes on Shannon. He could see that Shannon was deeply troubled and that he could not fault him for.

"Shannon, may we pray with you?" Richard waited patiently for Shannon to control his emotions and nod. "It's what we do, pray for one another. At a time such as this, even though we work in security, we still need to seek the protection of our God for these two."

"Thank you, Richard, Stephen. That is so appreciated." Shannon brushed as his eyes as the two other men tried to hide their emotions.

Stephen was on his feet when they finished with their prayers, returning with pads of paper and pens. Shannon frowned at them, his eyes stopping on Richard's face. Richard grinned and shrugged.

"We don't know Sorley, Shannon. We have seen him around church but I don't know that we have really spoken to him other than just in passing. We need your help to understand who he is, his friends, your family. Anything that would help us."

"Help to find him?" Shannon sighed, knowing that he had to do that but at a loss to really describe his son. He began to speak, his words listened to by the other two men, who made notes, sharing an occasional glance.

"Shannon, you're from this town?" Stephen's pen was lifted as he studied his notes.

"We're from the country outside of here, actually. Both Sari and I were raised in the country. We live closer to Oak City where we attend church and all that." Shannon sipped at his coffee, a frown on his face.

"I see. But Sorley lives here. What does he do for hobbies?"

"Hobbies? Reading. Running. Nature. He likes to garden. Anything that will get him outside."

"Similar to Silver." Richard was on his feet, heading for the door. He stepped back as Bill appeared and watched as Timothy and Naomi walked towards them.

"Timothy? Where's Tate?"

"She's with Mae. They had plans for the night, they tell me, and she told me to get lost." Timothy grinned, seeing the grin on Tate's face as she said that.

"Got kicked out, did you?" Richard gave a low laugh. "Wait until you two marry. She won't do it then."

"I don't mind if she does. She needs that friendship with the ladies." He peered towards the kitchen, hearing a voice that he didn't recognize. "Who's here?"

"Shannon, Sorley's father. He is helping us to understand his son seeing as we don't know him."

"No, we don't. But Jason Long would be a good one to talk with. He and Sorley are friends."

"I see. And Jason is working the investigation. Let's talk to Bill about that. For now, come on through and see what we can come up with."

Bill stood near the counter, listening to the conversation around him. He walked outside, trying to process what he had heard. He turned as he heard footsteps as he stood on the porch.

"Bill? Any word?" Naomi's voice held hope.

"Not a word, Naomi. There is just no sign of them. It's like they were transported somewhere to another planet." Bill was frustrated at that.

"It does, doesn't it?" Naomi pulled out her phone, frustrated at its' constant chiming. She frowned before she was reaching for Bill's arm, pulling him away from the house.

"Naomi?"

"Bill? Read this!" She almost threw her phone at him.

Bill frowned, not sure what Naomi was up to. His eyes dropped to her phone as he read the text before he was looking up.

"Where did this come from?"

"I don't know. I don't know that number. Is it true? Does he really know where they are?"

Bill forwarded the text to the lab, with a message asking that they track it.

"He might. Come on. We need to talk to Richard and the others. Please, Lord, let this be true."

Bill and Naomi ran for the house, startling the others as they flew through the house door, Richard on his feet, a question dying on his lips as he took Naomi's phone.

—

33

Chapter 6

"Bill?" Richard's voice held hope. "Is this true?"

"I have no idea. I have the techs tracing it. We need to make some plans, Richard. Shannon? What is your occupation?"

"Me? I'm a retired officer. Right now, I'm working at a bookstore just for something to do." Shannon's face was stern. "Why are you asking?"

"Because Naomi received a text that said someone knows where Silver and Sorley are. We have to confirm this before we can even think about moving in to rescue them."

Shannon nodded, knowing that Bill was speaking the truth.

"It has never sat well with me that they were not in the quarry. You would't remember, it's grown up so much, but it was a source of a series of drug raids a few years ago. There are still rumours going around that there are grow ops in there. Is that why?"

Bill nodded. He had heard the same rumours.

"It's possible but we need to determine if they are there. If they're not, then we need to find them."

Stephen reached for Naomi's phone, sending the text to himself. He then was on his feet, heading for Richard's computer. Naomi followed him, quiet conversation between then.

"Naomi? How did you get that text?"

"I have no idea, Stephen." Naomi paced as she waited for Stephen to finish his search. "What did you find?"

"That number is unlisted, as we thought. Now, that place? It's outside of the quarry, but it could be a red herring, now couldn't it?" Stephen sat back, his eyes on the computer monitor. "I know Richard. He'll want to head out there tomorrow."

"And we can't. We have that person in that we have to provide security for." Naomi was frustrated.

"We do. Who can we talk with?" Stephen looked over towards the hall, hearing Bill and Richard arguing. "What's up with that?"

Naomi headed for the kitchen before she was back.

"Bill knows who owns the place and won't tell Richard. Call Samuel." Samuel, a close friend, was a title searcher.

"I already have." Stephen had taken a chance that Samuel would be available and had heard back from him that he would give it priority.

They heard the door shut loudly and then were on their feet to head for Richard.

"Richard?" Naomi's voice broke into his thoughts. "What was that all about? You and Bill never argue."

"No, we don't. This time we did." Richard's eyes were on Shannon. "Shannon?"

Shannon shrugged, not sure if he should say anything.

"Bill is under a lot of pressure, Richard, not just from this." Shannon knew only too well what it was like. "He needs to take a break but he won't."

"No, he won't. He's been through this too many times." Timothy paced, his phone out as he stepped outside. He just needed to speak with his lady. "Tate? How are you?" A smile lit up his face.

"Timothy? You're not supposed to be calling me!" Tate's laughter reached through to him, easing his thoughts.

"I know. I just needed to speak with you. Are you and Mae enjoying yourselves?"

"We are. But you needed to ask something."

"I do. Is Mae near you?"

"She is. Let me put you on the speaker phone."

"Timothy? What do you need?" Mae was also a retired officer.

"The quarry. Sorley's father is here. He's retired officer too. He mentioned the rumours about the quarry and grow ups. I think I can remember that from when I was a teen but I thought it was too overgrown for that."

"It is really overgrown but there are areas that would work for that. Is that what you're thinking? That they saw something?"

"Maybe. Right now, we're grasping at straws. I could see something happening to them because of that."

"It is true." Mae was pacing, a hand rubbing at her face. "Let me reach out to some friends who are on a federal task force for drugs. Bill's brother is on that as well. Wesley may have information that."

"I'm sure that he will, now that it has been brought up. We'll see what happens there. I'll let you ladies get back to your fun times. Tate, I'll call later." Timothy pocketed his phone, his head turning as Stephen approached. "I just spoke with Mae."

"Mae? And she has friends who can help."

"She mentioned Bill's brother."

"Wesley? Why?" Stephen stared at his friend before his eyes slid closed. "The drug task force?"

"That's right. He's still working on that. We need to reach out to him."

"We will. Bill likely will as well. Let's go find Richard and see what he has to say." Stephen hesitated. "Samuel?"

Timothy nodded, knowing what Stephen was asking.

"I sent him a text. He's willing to work it for us."

"That's good. Now, what will Richard have for us to do? At least, we only have that one person tomorrow and that's it for the week. We won't be doing our training, that's for certain."

"No, we won't. We'll be looking for Silver."

Richard looked up from his notes, listening to Shannon as he spoke his thoughts aloud. He gave a brief nod as Timothy simply shook his head. They were not sure on Shannon as yet but they did trust him.

—

Chapter 7

Richard stood two days later, his eyes on the quarry. He had managed to reach out to Bradon from the Barnabas Foundation and Bradon had appeared, Kade in tow.

"Where do you want to start, Richard?" Bradon was not familiar with the quarry.

"I'm not sure. Mae, a friend, has given me a map a friend of hers made but it's a few years old." Richard handed over a copy. "This is what we have. We think that they were hidden here but we don't know for sure if they were or still are. It's really overgrown." He looked down at Kade, a beautiful Australian Shepherd.

"Kade will work what he can. We'll see what we can find for you." Bradon walked off, Kade on his working leash, Timothy and Stephen flanking him.

Naomi watched them and then turned to Richard, her head tilting to study him.

"Richard? What are your thoughts? You've been quiet."

"I know. I am trying to stay positive, Naomi, but it is hard."

"It is, Richard. This is where your own pep talks about God are repeated to you. You know only too well what is ahead of them. What can I do to help?"

"You're doing that by being you. You're praying and that helps. Other than that, just continue what you're working on." Richard paced away, his emotions overcoming him for a moment. Silver was special to them all, a bright light in the darkness that they worked in at times.

Naomi watched Richard, praying for him and also for protection for her friend. Silver was like a sister to her, more than just a fellow employee and friend. She was afraid, she had to admit, that Silver would not come back.

Timothy turned as Bradon stopped, his eyes narrowing as he watched Kade. Kade seemed to be picking up on something. Timothy just wasn't sure what it was. Stephen stopped beside him.

"He's found something, I think." Stephen's voice was low, not wanting to disturb Bradon's concentration.

"I think so. I just pray that it's them."

"You and me both."

Bradon beckoned them forward, his eyes on Kade.

"Fellows? Kade has picked up on something on this trail. It's well used and not by animals. Those are human tracks."

Timothy nodded.

"That they are. Do we follow it or not?"

"We can for a while. I don't like it though." Kade was tugging at his leash and Bradon moved after him.

Timothy and Stephen exchanged a glance and then shrugged. They followed Bradon, intent on watching for any danger. They came to an abrupt stop as Bradon halted, his hand on Kade's head. Kade gave a low whine, looking up at Bradon for a moment before his attention was focused back on the ramshackle shed in front of them. It could not be called a cabin even though it was that big.

"Bradon?" Timothy's voice was low. "What's Kade picking up on?"

"Someone is in there. I can't tell if it's your friends or not. It may well be." Bradon turned to watch the area around him. "I don't sense that we have someone here watching us. We need to get in and out and do that quickly."

Timothy nodded, his head bowing as he prayed. Stephen followed his example, their prayers for their friends and that they would find them here and get them to safety.

The two men moved forward as Bradon walked the perimeter of the small clearing, Kade's hackles slightly raised. He sensed danger as he gave low growls.

Timothy and Stephen hesitated at the door, their eyes meeting before Timothy's hand reached for the door, landing flat against it. He hesitated for a moment, his prayer once more asking that Silver would be here. He shoved open the door, catching it as it almost fell. Stephen looked at him and shrugged. The door hung on only one badly rusted hinge.

They waved hands in front of their faces as dust flew through the air, dust that they had disturbed simply by opening the door. They stepped inside,

———

coughing for a moment, coughing that they could not help. They searched the dim room, lit only from the sunlight that came through the open door before Timothy gave a cry and sprang forward. He was on his knees beside the still form, a hand reaching for Silver. Stephen dropped to the other side, reaching to roll Sorley to his back.

"They've been hurt, Timothy." Stephen looked around, on his feet again to search the cabin. He frowned at the implements that he found. *They were right,* he thought. *This has to be connected to a grow-op of some kind.*

"Let's move, Stephen." Timothy reached to help draw Sorley to his feet, finding him almost as tall as they both were. Stephen had Sorley over his shoulder and headed for the door, hearing Timothy behind him, knowing that Silver would be in his arms.

Bradon spun as he heard noise and pointed silently towards the trail. Kade's hackles were raising higher and he stopped Bradon's forward track. Bradon looked around, hoping to find another path and then pointed to their left. The three men moved quickly that way, disappearing from view onto another path, not quite as well worn but still travelled. Kade surged again, tugging Bradon forward as fast as he could move. He knew that the other two men were behind him. He just prayed that they would be able to get away and get these two to safety. His friends at the Barnabas Foundation had gathered during this time to pray for him and the safe recovery of Silver, a friend to all of them but particularly their wives.

———

The three men paused for a moment as they hit the path before they were away almost on a run. They were not that far from the parking lot, they could tell. Once there, Silver and Sorley were tucked into a vehicle and Timothy drove off. Stephen waited with Bradon, his phone out to call Richard.

"Richard?" Stephen could hear the sounds of nature in the call. Richard was outside, he decided. "We have them. Timothy is headed in with them."

Richard hesitated before he spoke.

"You have them? They're alive?" He waited, almost afraid to breathe.

"They are. They're in rough shape but alive. Head that way. I'm still here at the quarry with Bradon. I'm calling Bill."

"Do that. I'll head over to the hospital. Naomi is here with Tate and Mae." Richard nodded at the question on Naomi's face, seeing her face light up as she realized that Silver was safe.

Richard pocketed his phone, reaching for each of the ladies to hug them before his head was down and he was praying for his friends.

"They're alive?" Tate wasn't quite sure.

"They are, Tate. Your guy is headed in with them. Stephen is still at the quarry. Come on. We'll head over there and then I'll catch up with Stephen."

—

Chapter 8

Stephen turned as he heard vehicles, not surprised to see patrol vehicles with Bill. He had expected that.

"Stephen? I didn't expect this. They're safe?" Bill nodded at Bradon, his eyes on Kade for a moment.

"They are. We didn't wait to call for help. Timothy took off with them. Not the best move but we had no choice. There were men moving in towards the cabin." Stephen pointed behind him. "I'll show you the path and then leave it for you." He walked towards the trail, worry for his friend uppermost in his mind.

Bill nodded and walked the path, officers following him, their hands on their holstered weapons. They had no idea what faced them. They were all experienced men and women on the force and used to facing danger.

Holding up his hand, Bill frowned. He could hear conversation from the cabin, loud yells and then the sound of something breaking. He nodded drawing his weapon and moved forward, confident in the officers with him. He stood, his head tilting before he moved through the door. Officers moved in behind him, startling the two men standing there.

Bill simply shook his head as the men were handcuffed and then shoved from the cabin. He kept a number of officers with him, searching the cabin. They could see evidence of Silver and Sorley being kept there. He frowned for a moment as he turned, heading for the door. They should have been able to escape. He wanted to know why they hadn't.

"Stephen?" Bill approached his friend. "What condition were they in?"

Stephen shook his head, not quite sure what Bill was asking.

"They were unconscious, Bill. Huddled together for warmth I would think." Stephen's mouth worked as he fought his emotions. "They are shackled, Bill, at their ankles. Someone did this."

Bill stared at him, horror briefly on his face.

"Shackles? Both of them?" At Stephen's nod, Bill paced away and then was back at Stephen's side. "Come with me. Bradon?"

Bradon shook his head.

"I'll give someone at your detachment my statement. Then I'm heading home. I have a commitment today that I won't miss." Bradon walked away, Kade pacing at his side, his watchfulness now gone.

"Come on, Stephen. I need to head for the hospital. I'm sure there are officers there."

"Andrew called. He was heading that way." Stephen's head went back on the headrest. He was exhausted, he knew, having spent long hours working and then searching for Silver.

"Stephen, talk to me. Tell me what you saw." Bill's voice roused him from his thoughts.

———

"You saw it, Bill. You saw how bad it was. They were unconscious in the middle of the floor. Huddled together as if to stay warm. We didn't see anyone but we did hear someone moving in."

Bill nodded, knowing that Stephen was correct.

"You were right, Stephen. We've arrested two men who were there. Not the brightest bulbs on the tree."

Stephen gave a quick grin, watching as Bill parked near the Emergency Department of the hospital.

"Richard was heading this way, he said." Stephen hesitated for a moment, not sure where to head.

"Go find him, Stephen. I'll come looking for you soon." Bill watched with compassion as Stephen nodded and then walked away, a slump to his shoulders. Bill sighed, his heart raised in prayer for his friends. This was where they had to depend on God. Trusting in situations was hard, he knew only too well.

Richard looked around as Stephen stopped beside him. He frowned at the look on Stephen's face. The look matched that on Timothy's.

"Stephen? Timothy hasn't said anything. Can you?"

Stephen nodded, reaching to hug Naomi and then Tate. He stood for a moment, fatigue making him sway. Naomi's arm around him had him nodding before he sat. A cup of coffee appeared in his line of sight.

Richard walked away for a moment, seeing the physician waiting for him.

"Richard? You can come back." The physician, Joe Black by name, was a friend from church. "Silver hasn't roused yet. Her family asked if I would find you."

"Thanks, Joe. What about Sorley?"

"His parents are with him. You can stop in there too, if just for a few moments."

Richard nodded, stopping for a moment at the room where Silver was. He didn't like this. Silver was an integral part of his team and also a good friend.

Saul turned as he heard footsteps, his hand reaching to shake Richard's.

"Richard? Thank you."

Richard shrugged, his eyes on Silver.

"How is she?"

"They're still assessing her. She's battered some. Dehydrated. And then there are the shackles."

"Shackles?" Richard looked at Meg as she reached to hug him.

"They were shackled, Richard." Saul looked around as Seamus moved behind him.

"Shackled. Like prisoners." Seamus was frustrated. His sister had been kidnapped and kept captive. He was worried about her as well.

Richard shook his head and then focused on Silver. He reached to touch her face and then walked away. She needed time with her family. He needed time with his God. He sought out the chapel, not ready to face his team again. He would draw the strength that he needed from the Source that he always ran to and then find his friends.

Chapter 9

Rousing at last, Silver rolled to her side, a frown on her face as she felt the softness of the mattress and the warmth of the blankets over her. She heard the sounds that are common in a hospital and then cracked open her eyes. She stared around in wonder. She was in a hospital? How did that happen?

She sat up, not finding her head spinning as she had anticipated. She threw back the covers, scooted off the bed and reached for the bag of clothes sitting on a chair. Dressing quickly, Silver moved from her room, searching for Sorley. She paused at his door, seeing that he was alone. Walking quietly forward, Silver stood for a moment before her hand was out to touch his face, seeing the ravages of what they had been through on it. She had worried about him, worried that he was hurt worse than she knew. He hadn't roused, not that she was aware of. Her thoughts drifted back to the time in the cabin before she shuddered with fear.

Sorley stirred, feeling something touching him. He swiped at his face, feeling a hand touch his and then grip it. He sighed. *Who was this, who touched me? I don't know of a lady who would other than Mom. This is not what she would do.*

His eyes squinting against the low light, his headache raged. He had not been able to relieve it and had spent most of the last few days sleeping. He had awakened briefly and helped to his feet and then back to the floor. Sorley vaguely remembered a lady being there. He worried about her.

"Sorley? Are you going to ever wake up?" Silver's worried voice reached through the darkness that threatened him once more.

"I'm awake. Who are you?" His head rolled that way as he frowned at her.

"I'm Silver. We were kidnapped a few days ago. Someone must have found us, though. We're in the hospital."

"We are?" Sorley shoved himself up on his elbows, regretting that for a moment. "Can we leave?"

"I don't think so. You need medical help."

"No, I don't." Sorley's voice had the petulant tone of a child denied what he wanted to do. He sighed. "I'm sorry. I didn't mean it that way. But I want to leave. I don't do hospitals."

"You don't? Neither do I." Silver looked around, startled to hear footsteps. "Stephen? What are you doing here?"

Stephen grinned, knowing that Silver was trying to make a getaway and that Sorley wanted to go along.

"Looking for you two. Richard's outside, getting your discharge papers. We're taking you two home to his place for the next couple of days. And yes, both your families will be there. Scoot out of here, Silver, while I help your guy get dressed." He grinned at the glare sent his way.

Silver stood outside the room, her eyes on Richard as he walked towards her. She was simply wrapped into a hug and a prayer whispered in her ear.

"I am so glad to see you here, Silver. We were all so worried." Richard stepped back, assessing her. He knew that she shouldn't be leaving the hospital but that there was no way that they could or would stop her.

"Thank you, Richard. I don't remember a whole lot other than the first bit. Bill was around and took what I could give him." She looked towards the closed door. "Sorley was hurt."

"We know that, Silver. And he will heal. Stephen tell you where we're heading?"

"He did. But our families?" Silver didn't want that. She would feel smothered. Her father and brother had a habit of doing that although she could and would put them down when she needed to. They just stared at her from the ground where they had landed. They always forgot not to test her too far.

"We'll bring them in later this morning. They need to see you, Silver. They need to know for themselves that you are okay. We can tell them that. The physicians and medical staff can tell them that. But until they speak with you and see you on your feet, they really won't believe it."

Silver sighed, knowing that Richard spoke the truth.

"Who found us?" She thought that she had been told but couldn't remember for sure.

"Timothy. Stephen. And Bradon and Kade helped track down the shack. Bill was surprised that they found you."

"We were well hidden, I guess. I need to know what you know, Richard. I have to know that." Silver watched closely as the door opened and Sorley appeared, his arm clasped lightly in Stephen's grip.

"We will talk, Silver. First though, we get you to my place and then to bed. You both need that. We all do. Once you've had a chance to get some sleep and get some food into you, then we'll talk. I promise. Bill and Lily will be there. He's already asked for that. Andrew has weighed in also."

Silver nodded grumpily. She just want to go somewhere and hide and couldn't. She knew that. Her family wouldn't let her. Her friends wouldn't let her. And her team most certainly would stay close to her. She just didn't know if she could handle that.

Sorley's eyes closed as he laid down on another bed, not feeling the shoes pulled from his feet or the blanket pulled over him. Stephen left on a low light, standing and watching Sorley for a moment. As the paramedic on the team, he had spoken with the physicians the night before just to get an understanding onwhat they faced. He had sought and obtained consent for that from both Silver and Sorley.

Richard watched for a moment, knowing that Naomi was with Silver and was getting her settled. He could hear low conversation from that room.

"Richard? He's asleep again. I don't think that he should have come out yet."

—

"Not likely." Richard yawned, fatigue weighing him down. "Go and get some sleep, Stephen. I'll wake you in a couple of hours."

Naomi headed his way, tears in her eyes. She shook her head as she passed him, heading for another bedroom and some sleep. She was worried about Silver and would until they had found whoever it was. What little Silver had muttered had disturbed her.

Chapter 10

Rousing early the next morning, Silver refused to open her eyes. She just wanted to stay in bed and not face anyone. She didn't have the answers that she knew they would want. Her thoughts turned to prayer and then to praise. God had provided for herself and Sorley, freeing them. She could still feel the shackles around her ankles. That scared her. Silver wasn't sure if she would even recover from that but knew that it would take time.

On her feet, she reached for the clothes that Naomi had left for her. One shower and some clean clothes later, Silver hesitated with her hand on the door knob. She would need to face her team and then face Sorley. She sighed. And her family would be around at some point. *How do I do this, Lord? How do I find the answers and yet keep them safe? They will want to be here and I don't want that.*

Richard turned as he heard her footsteps, watching her intently, assessing her as best he could. He needed her at full strength for the next week when they had to be away on a security assignment. He just wasn't sure that she would be.

"Richard? Thank you." She walked past him, intent on a cup of coffee.

"You're welcome, Silver. We need to talk." Richard sat down across from her, his mug hitting the table.

"We will. Just not right now." Silver was feeling grumpy. She opened her mouth to apologize, snapping it shut as Richard shook his head.

"How is Sorley?" Silver looked towards the hallway.

"He's still sleeping. Stephen has been in and out over the last few hours. He needs that, Silver. We'll wake him up in a while."

Silver nodded, her thoughts drifting.

"What do you want to know, Richard? I did talk to Bill."

"Tell me what you can." Richard looked past her as Timothy and Tate and Naomi appeared. "We need to know what you went through in order to understand how to help you."

Silver nodded, returning the hugs from her friend, her eyes on the hallway once more as she heard footsteps. Sorley appeared in the doorway. Silver was on her feet, moving into his space and into his hug. *He's alive, Lord. Thank you. Now, please Lord, help us to solve this quickly so that we can move on.*

Sorley simply held her, content to have her in his arms. He had sensed her presence over the past few days, trying her best to take care of him. He just wasn't sure how hurt that she had been.

"Silver? You're okay?" He rested his chin on the top of her hair, his eyes closing. He didn't see the speculative looks sent their way.

"I am, I think. How about you? You scared me." Silver didn't want to move.

"I did? I don't remember."

"No, you won't. You were out of it most of the time." Silver sighed, knowing that she had to move and not wanting to. She felt as if she had come home.

"I was, I guess. Now, introduce me to your friends. I know I've seen them around." He released her and gently turned her to face the five facing them.

"I can do that." Silver didn't move, feeling Sorley's hands on her shoulder. "Richard, I think you met last night. He is our team leader. Stephen was the one who helped you. The lady next to him is Naomi. And then there's Timothy and his lady, Tate."

Sorley nodded, watching each one carefully. He was being assessed, he knew and quietly took it, confident in the lady in front of him that her friends would not find him wanting.

"Sorley? Come and sit. We'll feed you. Then we'll pray. It's something that we do, pray together as friends and as a team."

Sorley sank into a chair, feeling Silver's hand on his shoulder as he did so. He reached to pull her down to the chair beside him. He took with a quiet word of thanks the food handed to him.

Stephen and Timothy shared a look, before their gaze turned to Silver. She was concentrating on her food. They could see that she was troubled.

Tate reached for Silver's hand, giving a squeeze before she was on her feet. She moved away, Timothy watching her closely. She was troubled by what had happened to Silver. Her adventure was still too fresh in her mind to rest easy about her friend.

Richard turned at last to Sorley and Silver, his hand reaching for the pad of paper and pen that he had handy.

"Talk to us, Silver. Tell us what happened."

Silver nodded, her eyes on him.

"First, Richard, tell us how you knew that we were missing. Bill said our vehicles are missing."

"They are. Bill has someone actively looking for them. He has reached out to the towns around us as well." Richard tapped his pen against the paper. "We're trying to find them as well."

"They've likely scrapped them. I'll need to talk to the insurance company about that."

"You do and so does Sorley." Richard paused for a moment, his eyes narrowing for a moment. "Go on, Silver."

"I don't know who took us. It was just so strange."

Silver started from when they had been approached until she had lost consciousness. She had awakened briefly at one point, shivering with the cold. She had shifted closer to Sorley without knowing that she had.

At one point, she had roused and stood, staring around. She attempted to take a normal step, tripping and falling hard to her hands and knees. The breath was knocked from her. Silver shifted around to a

57

sitting position, not sure what she had tripped on. She reached for her ankles, feeling the metal. *What is this,* she thought? *Who did this? I don't remember getting here and I don't remember these. How do I get away if this is what happened?*

Hearing a noise, Silver froze for a moment and then shifted once more. She stared around, not seeing what could only be heard as a groan torn from a human. Her eyes dropped and she stopped moving once more. Back on her hands and knees, she crawled towards the form. A hand out to touch him confirmed that he was indeed a person and alive. She frowned at him before her brow cleared. *This was Sorley,* she thought. *Sorley was hurt and needed care. She could care for him if only she had what she needed and until someone came and found them and got them to healthcare help.*

—

Chapter 11

Silver had struggled to her feet, balancing for a moment until she felt that she could stand steadily. She searched the cabin or rather shack for water and a cloth. She had looked with disgust at the cloths that she found, not even wanting to touch one. They were all that dirty. Silver looked back towards Sorley before she reached for a bottle of water. She would do what she could.

Raising his head slightly, she was able to get him to drink before she drank some herself. She then poured water along the side of his head, the hem of her T-shirt used to wipe away as much blood as she could. She refused to use the cloths that were in the cabin. She sat, her eyes searching the cabin, a hand resting on Sorley's chest. She knew that he was back into unconsciousness even if he had roused slightly as she wiped at the blood. He had not stayed with her and that frightened her. Not much frightened Silver who was known for being fearless in her work on the security team. This was personal, though, and that made a difference.

She wasn't too sure afterwards how long that she had sat there, her thoughts muddled, trying to make sense of what had happened. She just couldn't. The door scraping open caused her to jump but she never looked around.

The man who entered, shriveled, shrunken, and stooped, paused before he just walked by her. The evilness of how he lived was graven in his face. He

---

turned, cruel eyes on Silver and then Sorley. He thought that they would have been on their feet by now. It was obvious that they weren't. He had orders to put them to work in the evil operation that he was in charge of. He couldn't if they were not upright.

He walked over, his foot out and kicking at Sorley's ribs, causing the younger and healthier man to groan with a hand finding the spot. Silver had jumped and then jumped to her feet, yelling at the man to leave Sorley alone. She didn't back down when he stalked around the body to stand in front of him. That shocked him. Everyone always moved away from him or looked away. She did neither. A hand came out, slamming across her face and sending her to the floor where she lay motionless. He shrugged and walked away, the bar on the door dropping across it to lock them in. He would be back on the morrow. They just needed to be on their feet.

The next few days were the same. Silver's face ached from the blow. Yet, she was more worried about Sorley. She helped him to his feet every few hours, watching as he stumbled around the room, trying to escape or find comfort. His words were mumbling.

Sorley rested at one point, sitting back on the floor, an arm around Silver. He was out of breath, his head pounding, and his vision blurring. He had no idea where they were. He had heard the shouts of the man whenever he returned, tucking away his words for when he was more awake and could remember them. He needed to get Silver away, he knew, but he also knew that he just couldn't. He had heard the words "grow-op" and grew afraid. Sorley slumped back to

—

60

the floor, taking Silver with him. Neither one of the couple moved, Silver tucked close to Sorley as he sought to protect her.

Neither one of them heard the door scrape open the morning before. They didn't hear the footsteps of the men who entered or the sounds of dismay as they were discovered. Neither Sorley or Silver felt themselves gathered up and carried away to help

Silver came back to the present, her eyes on Sorley who was in turn focused solely on her. Her eyes were puzzled at the look in his, not sure what was happening. She just knew that she was tied to this man in a way that she was not tied to the others. She needed space to get her head back on straight. Her team mates just wouldn't let her, not at present at any rate.

"I think that's it, Richard. I can't remember a lot." Silver shifted her gaze to her boss.

"We'll work with what we have. Sorley?" Richard's question caught Sorley off guard.

Sorley jumped at the suddenness of Richard's question. He shrugged.

"Silver would know more than I do. I can't remember a whole lot." He looked down at Silver for a moment as she snorted. "Silver?"

"You weren't awake. How could you remember?"

Sorley stared at her before his eyes narrowed. He caught the slight look of humour in her eyes.

"And you were awake the whole time?" He grinned suddenly as she shook her head. "Didn't think so." They were oblivious of the looks that they were garnering.

"Richard, was there a grow-op out there?" Silver shifted her thoughts to what the man had said. "The man was muttering something about making us work in one. Or else making us work in a drug factory somewhere. What did we stumble into?"

"Bill didn't say if there was one. He may not be able to say, even though you have been threatened that way. I have heard the same rumours." Richard looked towards Timothy. "Timothy? Has Mae said anything?"

Timothy shrugged, having had a similar conversation with Mae.

"She has heard the same rumour. Neither one of us could confirm them. I've reached out to our friends to see what they can come up with. Emma's away but said that she'd work on it as soon as she could."

Stephen had been watching the couple across from him, a frown appearing on his face.

"Sorley, what do you do?"

"What do I do? For work?" At Stephen's nod, Sorley rubbed at his face, finding the sore spot on the side of his head. "I work in finance. I am registered as a financial analyst but I do more than that. I know that I can trust you. I work with law enforcement in tracking finances on those suspected of hiding financials here in Canada but more importantly overseas." He looked around as he heard an united sound from the group. "What did I say?"

"Just what you did." Richard nodded at him. "If someone wanted to discredit you, they could do that by making you work in something illegal even for an hour. That would make all your work suspect."

Silver was nodded as well.

"That's true, Richard." Sorley had turned to watch her, reaching for her hand without thinking of what he had done. "We've seen in it before. That would taint you and then taint any investigation that you had been part of. Do you usually run out there?"

Sorley shrugged.

"I do every couple of weeks. Anyone following me would know that." He paled, his mouth tightening into a grim line. "Someone has been following me. What case am I working on that would be affected?"

"Or what case will you be asked to investigate?" Tate spoke up, knowing that she had to.

"You're right, Silver." Richard paced, his thoughts troubled. "Sorley, how do you find work?"

"Find work? You mean, how do I find what I investigate? I am usually contacted by a law enforcement agency. I speak with them and then decide if I want to take on the case or not. I can refuse if I wish."

Chapter 12

Hours later, Sorley walked through his house, his brother watching him. Sean hesitated at first about bringing him home, watching the connection between his brother and Silver. He could not say no, though, when he was asked to bring his brother back to his own home.

"Sorley? What really happened?" Sean reached to steady his brother as he turned quickly and then fought to stay on his feet.

"I'm not sure. I know that I had gone there to run, found Silver, and then it's pretty much a blank. She tells me that I was knocked out by a weapon butt." Sorley rubbed at his head. "I don't remember being in that shack as she called it."

"That's what she said. I just was hoping, I guess, that you had remembered something else." Sean turned from his brother, heading for the door. He opened it to find his parents there, simply pointing to the living room.

Saul headed that way, Meg for the kitchen. Sean followed his mother, his eyes watchful. He felt worry for his brother and then for Silver. He knew her from church from a Bible study group that he could sometimes attend.

"Sean, how is he?" Meg turned from setting her parcels on the counter, reaching to hug her youngest son.

"He's on his feet, Mom, but still really rocky. He shouldn't be by himself. He's refusing to come to either of our homes."

"And you have decided to stay here?" Sean's nod had his mother nodding in return.

"I have, Mom." His eyes narrowed at the look on her face. "And so have you."

"We will, Sean. We need to whether he wants it or not." Meg hesitated, not sure how to ask what she needed to. "This Silver? Where is she?"

"Silver? She goes to our church, Mom. She is also on Richard's security team."

"She works for Richard? I didn't know that. Does Sorley?"

"He does, Mom. We were there today. Richard met with us." Sean turned as he heard Sorley's voice raised slightly. "What is going on? Sorley?"

Sorley stared at his brother and then shook his head. He stalked away, the door closing behind him. Sinking to the steps on the back porch, Sorley buried his head in his hands. He didn't want his parents there. He worried too much that his mother might be hurt. And he didn't want that. How did he get them to stay away?

Not moving as he heard the door open and then close, Sorley simply sat. He felt someone sit beside him, the faint scent of roses letting it know it was his mother. He sighed to himself.

"Sorley, we understand that you don't want us around you. We understand that you are worried.

We're not leaving you on your own. You know that we won't. We're not in law enforcement. However, you are our son, our oldest. We love you dearly, son. We don't want to see you hurt any more. And we understand that you are worried about about us. We will not stay away. Live with that." Her arm was around him, her prayer audible to them both.

Sorley had stiffened when Meg first began to speak and then relaxed. He knew his family would be around whether he wanted them or not.

"Thanks, Mom. I do want to keep you safe." Sorley dropped a kiss on his mom's cheek. "How do I do this?"

"With God's help, son. He will protect us. We may not like what you have to go through, but He will guide and lead you. I know also that you will not walk away from this young lady." Meg watched her son's face, seeing a slight softening on it as he thought of the young lady as she referred to her as.

"I know that, Mom. It's just that she's already been hurt because of me. And I don't want that to happen any more."

"We know that, son. It is out of your hands, though. I don't think that Silver will stay away from you. Not from what I understand from Sean."

"Sean? He knows her?" Sorley turned his head to stare behind him, surprised to see his father and brother sitting there.

"I do, Sorley. Not real well. We're in a Bible study together when she's there." Sean studied his brother. "Can you say anything more about what happened?"

"If I could, I would. I just don't remember a lot." Sorley rubbed at his head. His headache was worsening.

Saul was on his feet and into the house, returning with the medications and water that his son needed. This was one time that he could not fix the problem, no matter how much that he wanted to.

Silver reached for her phone late that night. She had tried sleeping, but it just wasn't working. She had moved from her bed to her couch, cuddled under a blanket. She scrolled through her messages, smiles on her face from the ones her team mates had sent. Silver frowned at the one from Bill, knowing that they would need to meet the next day. Silas had sent one to simply say that he and Madigan were praying for her.

She paused as she reached the last message, her face softening as a smile lit her face. Sorley had sent a simple message to say good night and that he was praying for her. And then he asked if he could take her to lunch on the next day. Her fingers found the letters to respond before she set her phone to one side, her eyes closing as she slept.

Neither Sorley or Silver saw the men who wandered around their homes that night, seeking a way in. They both slept, their bodies needing that to refresh themselves. The men turned at last, frustrated at their inability to take these two captive again. That had been what their orders had been. They ducked down behind vehicles parked on the street as patrol cars moved past both houses, sent there by Bill to watch out for his friends.

Chapter 13

Sorley reached for Silver's hand the next day as they walked towards Ev's diner. He had appeared at her door not that long before, ready to spend some time with this lady who intrigued him. Silver looked down at their hands, shrugged, and simply walked beside him. This was not her, to hold hands with a man. In fact, she didn't date at all.

Seated in a booth, Silver waved at Andrew's cousin, Avery, who had appeared near them. Avery walked over, sitting beside Silver, his hand out to shake Sorley's.

"I am glad that you two are safe." Avery grinned at Silver's snort. They were old friends.

Sorley stared at him for a moment before his eyes narrowed at the smirk on Silver's face.

"Thank you, I think." He grinned as the two laughed at him. "Sorry, I'm still not thinking as clearly as I usually do." He reached for the menu and then dropped it. "Avery, you're in law enforcement. What do you know about that quarry?"

"Not a lot. It's always been rumoured of drugs being grown there. It has never been proven. It would be nice if we could do that." Avery was on his feet at that, returning to his tasks.

Silver shook her head. She knew that this was how Avery could be. He would think it through and then come to either her, Richard, or Andrew.

Sorley sighed, not sure what had just happened.

"Silver? You're on a security team. How do we do this?"

Silver sighed herself. She knew what he was asking. She just didn't have any answers.

"I'm not sure, Sorley. I think that we need to sit down with Richard and the others. We're out of town for the next week. I don't like that but it's what I do."

"It is. And I have to go back to work as well. I don't want to but it is what it is." He reached for the menu. "How be we eat and then find something fun to do? Unless you want to spend time with your family and friends." He waited for her response, genuinely wanting time with her.

"I would like that. I spoke with my parents and brother this morning. Richard also called but I don't need to touch base with him until tomorrow night. Now, let's eat. I'm starved."

The day passed quickly for them as they wandered the town, finding much in common. They had caught Bill's attention at one point. He had stood and watched them, shaking his head. Another couple, he thought, who found one another while they were in danger.

Silver turned the next morning as she stood just inside the church door. Seamus walked towards her, reaching to hug her.

"Silver? You're doing okay? No after effects from this week?"

Silver shook her head as she linked an arm with her brother.

"Let's find somewhere to sit, Seamus. Near the back, I think."

Seamus nodded, his eyes on Sorley as he approached them.

"Is Sorley sitting with us?"

"Sorley? Is he here?" Silver turned as he nodded behind her. Her face lit up. "Sorley? Where were you?"

"Right here. Waiting for you." He grinned at Seamus before reaching for Silver's hand. "We're sitting at the back."

Silver frowned at him even as she heard her brother laughing beside her.

"We are? And if I want to sit right up front?"

"You won't. You like the back. You told me that, remember?" Sorley grinned at her, waiting for Seamus to enter the pew before Silver followed. Neither of them caught the looks sent their way.

"I did, didn't I?" Silver's attention was on the front of the church, her eyes reading the verse that was showing on the wall at the front. *Thank you, Lord. I needed that reminder that You are in control and want only the best for me. I forget that too easily.*

Tate was watching her friend closely, Timothy's arm around her. She nodded towards them.

"Silver's here."

"She is?" Timothy looked around, catching Stephen's eye as he did so. Someone else was here, he knew, someone who was watching either Silver or Sorley or both of them. "She is and with Sorley."

"She is. They're a couple, just like we were." Tate shifted closer to her fiancé, welcoming the way his arm tightened on her.

"She is. And they are. I don't want to see them go through what we did."

"It's not in our hands, love. It's in God's. He allows this, just as He did for us. All we can do is pray for them. I worry about her."

"We all do. She can take care of herself in most cases. The other day was out of her control. And with Sorley hurt, she would have been torn about what to do."

"That's what she told me. It didn't help that she had a weapon pointed at her." Tate had had a long talk with Silver the night before, gently prying when Silver didn't want to speak.

"You've talked with her. Thank you."

Silver wandered her home that night. Her parents had been around, her mother helping her with the cleaning. It had been neglected since she returned home and she hated a dirty house. Her father had mown the lawn the day before. She was grateful for that. They took care of her, even though she lived on her own.

—

Sorley had called her, simply to say that he had enjoyed spending time with her that weekend and that he was praying for her. Would she just stay safe?

Silver had laughed, stating that she would and then asked if he would. He had grumbled at her before he had agreed to do so.

Chapter 14

Richard sank into his vehicle seat that following Friday. It had been a rough, tough week. Their client had tried their best to escape from the security net around them, not wanting to be kept safe. It had taken all the team's ingenuity and experience to keep the man safe.

The team was fatigued beyond what they had been before. They had looked at one another and then became quiet. Stephen steered the vehicle towards their home, his eyes on the road. He wanted to stay home after this, not having to deal with these people.

"Richard?" Timothy's voice sounded from the back seat. "Any more thoughts on what we've been discussing?"

Richard turned to watch Timothy.

"About what?"

"About doing what Abe does? Only not duplicating his training but training in what we've become experienced in?"

Naomi and Silver were nodding, watching Richard's face.

"I have. We need to meet, people. We're off on Monday. Let's plan on meeting on Monday to pray about this and then make some plans. I agree with you. This is getting old." Richard faced forward again, confident that God was working on this. He had had long talks with Abe and then Abe's men, garnering their feelings on change and how they saw where they were.

Silver sighed to herself. *This was indeed getting old,* she thought. *I pray that Richard does this. I want to stay here, stay home, and start a family. I can't do that if we're travelling all the time. And that would mean I would have to quit a job that I love.*

Sorley looked up as he heard a vehicle stopping near him and then the car door opening and closing. He was on his feet, reaching to hug Silver, holding on tight and not wanting to ever let her go.

"Sorley? You're here?" Silver was delighted to say the least.

"I am. I have food for us. Go on, sweetheart, and get changed. I'll head for your grill and start our meal. I just wanted to spend time with you. I missed you." He smiled down at her, seeing her face lighting up.

"That sounds wonderful, Sorley. Come on through the house. You'll find what you want in the cupboard on the porch." Silver danced away, her duffle bag swinging at her side. She was ecstatic. Sorley was here. She had wanted to see him so desperately. He had become her anchor over the last couple of weeks. She just didn't expect to see him so soon.

Sorley worked away, a grin on his face. Silver was home and unharmed. At least, he prayed that she was. He dropped the chicken breasts on the grill before he turned to the salad that he had concocted, setting it out with the dressings. He frowned before he nodded, heading for the kitchen and the dishes that were needed. He also reached to start a pot of coffee and then reached into the fridge for bottles of water. He wasn't sure which Silver would prefer.

Silver reached for clean clothes, the heat of the day driving her to find her favourite shorts and T-shirt, as faded as they were. She needed her comfort clothes, she decided, knowing that Sorley just wouldn't care.

Sorley turned once more, simply sweeping his lady into his arms and holding tight. He could feel how tight that she was holding on to him.

"Not a good week?" His voice was low, not wanting to disturb her. He felt her shaking her head. "That bad?"

"It was. It was one of the worst times that we have ever had. We've had people fight us before but not like this." Silver moved away from him, Sorley's arms dropping to his sides. She studied the table and then the grill before she turned back to him. Her emotions were raw at that moment.

Sorley reached for her again, just holding her, a prayer whispering over her. He could feel her relaxing against him.

"Let's eat, sweetheart. Then, we'll pray. We both need that." Sorley turned her to her chair, setting a plate in front of her before he was in his own chair. A hand reached for hers before a blessing was asked on their food.

Sorley kept the conversation light, his comments causing Silver to set aside her troubles. They helped

---

to lighten her night. She watched him closely, seeing his love for her shining in his eyes. She didn't think that he knew that he was that open but she felt loved, cherished, and safe.

Clearing the table, Sorley's hand kept Silver in her chair. He rinsed off their dishes, set them into the dishwasher, placed the remaining food into the fridge, and then reached to refresh their coffee. He walked back out to find Silver had moved down the yard, her eye searching the area for anything that should not be there. He simply walked towards her, his hand reaching for hers.

"Care to talk, sweetheart?" He waited patiently, knowing that she would speak when she was able to.

Silver shrugged, knowing that God was working in her life. She had felt Him doing that over the week. She sighed, thinking that was all that she was doing lately.

"It was a brutal week, Sorley. The client didn't want us there and fought us all the time."

"I'm sorry. It has to be hard keeping on doing what you do best." He led her to a swing in the back of the yard, shoving her down and sitting beside her, an arm wrapped around her to hold her tight to him.

"It is. Richard wants to meet on Monday." Her head went down on his shoulder, finding the comfort that he was offering her.

"He's thinking of changing what he does." Sorley didn't know this for sure but having spoken in depth with Richard, he felt he was on the right track with his words.

Silver nodded, hearing the sounds of nature in her ears. She could feel the slight breeze that was blowing and felt the warmth of the sun on her head. This was a favourite time of day for her when she could set aside everything and then relax, just spending time with her God.

"That sounds like a plan. Timothy has been grumbling, I know, wanting to be at home with Tate."

"We all want that. If and when we find the one God has for us, we don't want to be on the road. If there are children involved, we definitely don't want that." Silver settled down tighter to Sorley, not realizing how she was relaxing.

Their conversation was quiet, sparked with laughter before Sorley was on his feet, his hand reaching for hers.

"I need to get on the road, sweetheart. I'm glad that you're home. Now, come and lock up after me."

Silver leaned back against the door, her eyes closing for a moment. A tear trickled down her cheek. She had no idea why she was weeping but she was. Her emotions were in a turmoil, a large part because of the man who had just left. She was also deeply afraid, not certain that they were over with their adventure. Her fear was that they weren't and that Sorley would be hurt or even killed.

Chapter 15

The next morning, Richard stood in Bill's kitchen, Michael in his arms. Michael had simply held up his arms, knowing that the tall man standing in front of him would pick him up. Richard had been the recipient of a hug and sloppy kiss, a grin on his face. Cora was out and Bill had been watching Michael, loving the time with his son.

"Richard? You're troubled?" Bill pointed towards the table. "In here, I think."

"I am. On many fronts. How is the investigation into Silver and Sorley?" Richard sat, Michael wiggling to get down, intent on finding their cat who patiently waited for him to appear.

"It's not. We're at a loss. We've searched that area and didn't find anything. The men are not talking. They've been transferred to another jurisdiction."

Richard nodded, knowing that had been the case.

"I see. And yes, I am troubled. We had a horrible week this past week. I'm in need of your prayers, my friend."

"You're not quitting. You want to change. And your team wants that as well." Bill set a plate of food in front of Richard before setting his own plate on the table. He corralled his son and fastened him into the high chair, scrambled eggs and toast cut into small pieces set before him.

—

“We are, Bill. I would covet your prayers as we work through this.” Richard grew silent as they ate, Bill allowing him that.

“Okay, Richard. What can I do for you?” Bill cleared the table and sat back down, his eyes on his son for a moment.

Richard shrugged, his eyes on his hands.

“I am not sure, Bill. Your prayers help. We need to make decisions as a team or our team will splinter. None of us want that. We enjoy our work for the most part. I have conferred with Abe and his men and will continue to do so.”

Bill nodded, his thoughts on what Richard could do. He would think it through and provide Richard with his thoughts. That was what Richard was asking.

“We will do that. Now, about Silver and Sorley. How close are those two?”

Richard sighed, knowing what Bill was asking.

“I really don’t know. She’s being very quiet about it. And that’s not her. She is usually vocal about what is happening. She has never dated and has shown no interest in anyone. That doesn’t mean that there hasn’t been. This is different with Sorley. He’s interested in her and she’s responding. Part could be because of what they went through. A good part is God.”

“That it is. Now, as to where the investigation stands. I can’t share a lot, you know that. We’re actively searching for the man who held them captive.

———

80

We've searched that shack and the surrounding area without any success."

"And she has been watched. We've seen evidence of that, but not enough to bring in you or one of your officers. We've documented it all."

"Thanks, Richard. That is appreciated. Now, unless something else comes up, we have to set it aside. And that we don't want to."

"No, we don't." Richard sighed again as his phone vibrated. "Excuse me, Bill." He read the text and was on his feet. "I need to run, Bill. That was Silver. She's found a package."

Bill watched as Richard almost ran from the house. He couldn't leave, not with his son in the house, but he reached out to Lily, who was on duty that day.

Lily approached Sorley, who stood near Silver's home, behind the tape.

"Sorley?"

Sorley turned his head, his eyes on Lily.

"I don't know anything, Lily. I just arrived to find this. Richard was by and said that Silver reached out to him." Sorley was frustrated. He wanted to be with his lady but was prevented from that. He understood why, but it still didn't make it any easier.

Lily nodded, ducked under the police tape, and headed for the patrol officer who waited for her. She could see Silver standing nearby, her arms wrapped around herself. Lily searched the area for anyone who stood out, simply seeing Silver's concerned neighbours on their lawns and sidewalks watching for information.

"Pat? What do we have?" Lily walked towards the porch, a crime scene tech motioning to her.

"Silver found a package when she opened her front door. It was just sitting on the bottom step. She didn't disturb it." Pat walked besides Lily as she approached the house.

"Sam? What do we have?"

"Not a nice package, Lily." Sam turned back to the box. "It contains dead roses, a get lost card, and animal blood, we think."

"Animal blood?" Lily peered into the package. "Okay. Do what you need to. Make sure that Bill gets copied on everything."

"We will." Sam looked around at Silver, seeing her standing nearby, her face shuttered. "She's afraid, Lily."

"She is. After what they went through, she will be. We need to find this person and soon. What else?" Lily listened as she was updated on the investigation. She approached Silver at last, her head tilted to study her friend. "Silver?"

Silver jumped, her eyes huge in her face.

"I didn't hear you." Silver rubber at her arms, not sure what to say. "What was in it?"

"Dead roses. A get lost card. Animal blood." Lily reached out to steady Silver.

Silver was shaken, not having expected that. She frowned.

"A get lost card? Where would they get that?"

"I have no idea. I have never heard of one of those cards. They may have made it."

"I would suspect that they did." Silver watched Sorley, finding him watching her. Lily's gaze shifted between the two, not sure what to say.

"Silver? We'll be here for a while. Head off with Sorley. I'll find you."

Silver nodded before she walked towards Sorley, ducking under the tape that he held up, and into his arms. Sorley held her, feeling the shudders running through her before he turned her and walked her to his car. He tucked her away, finding Richard beside him.

"Take her somewhere, Sorley, and send me a text where you are. I'll stay here for now." Richard nodded towards Silver. "She's right on the edge and needs to get away from here."

Sorley nodded, finding his seat and driving away. He drove around aimlessly, not sure where Silver wanted to do.

<hr>

83

Silver walked through her home late that night. She had spent the day with Sorley and then her family, not talking much. Her family kept giving her those looks as she termed them. She just wanted this over and it wasn't. Lily had been around, discussing what was found but more to check in on her.

She reached for her Bible, needing to spend time with her God. She was afraid, she had to admit, and didn't know where to turn. Her family wanted to smother her. Her team members wanted to protect her. And Sorley? Her face softened as she thought of the man who was taking over so many of her thoughts and life. Yes, Sorley, he just wanted to protect her but let her live her life. He had simply stated that he would back her decisions, whatever they were, unless she was in danger. Then he would step in. He had left reluctantly that night, not wanting to leave her on her own.

Curling up on her couch, she read for a while and then slept. Her sleep was troubled and broken. That seemed to be the way it was with her lately. She slept late, not rising even when her phone chimed.

Sorley stared at his phone. Silver had not responded to his text as quickly as she usually did. He ran for his car, speeding towards her home, and then just sitting at the curb. Her car was here. She should be. He was out of his car and running for the front door. Pounding at it, Sorley waited for a response, not hearing anything. He kept pounding at the door,

---

terrified that Silver had disappeared and he wouldn't see her again.

Silver's head rose, her brain foggy for a moment. She frowned, trying to determine what had awakened her. The pounding at the door continued and she jumped. She stumbled to her feet, tangled as they were in her blanket, and fell. The jar of falling awakened her fully. She grumbled away as she untangled her feet and headed for the door. Yanking it open, she stared at Sorley, a frown on her face.

Sorley simply swept her into a hug and then back into the house, the door closing softly behind him. He held her as she sobbed, her emotions overwhelming her. He prayed for her and for their relationship. He wanted to protect her but knew that he couldn't do that, not when they weren't married.

Silver's tears finally halted, and she realized that Sorley was praying for her. She rested against him, not sure what to think. He had shown up when she needed him. She looked up at him, seeing his emotions in his eyes.

"Sorley?" Her voice was hesitant.

"Silver? I was so worried. I'm sorry. Did I wake you up?"

She nodded before stepping back from him.

"I need to change. I feel grubby." She squinted at him as he grinned. "It's not funny, buster."

"No, it's not, but you just look so cute." Without thinking, Sorley reached forward to kiss her forehead. "Head off, sweetheart. I'll start the coffee." He grinned at her as she frowned at him, thinking how adorable she was.

Sorley stood for a moment at the counter, his eyes on the clock. There was no way that they would make church on time. He didn't care. All he cared about was the lady who he had decided that he loved. Yes, he had finally acknowledged that to himself.

Silver watched Sorley, her heart on her face. She knew that she loved him and sensed that her love was returned. She was just not sure where they went from there.

"Sorley? It's too late for church, isn't it?"

Silver's voice startled Sorley who jumped slightly before he turned.

"It is. Come on out to the deck. We'll have our own church." Sorley reached to wrap an arm around her.

"We can. I think that we need to talk." Silver's voice was quiet, emotionless.

Sorley's heart dropped. She didn't want to see him any more. And he just couldn't do that. He was too worried about the danger that she was in. Well, and him too. She was that important to him.

Silver sat quietly, her hands clasped in her lap. She listened as Sorley prayed for them before she took up the petition. They needed to talk, she knew. She was just afraid that he would walk away from her. And the messages were coming at her fast and furious. She had finally muted her phone the night before to stop hearing them.

"Silver? We need to talk, sweetheart. But first, you're troubled."

"I am. I've been getting messages over the night. I muted my phone. I guess that's why I didn't hear you calling me." She stared past the porch railing, watching the butterflies and bees busy on the flowers.

"I thought that you had been. So have I. I've forwarded them on to Bill and Lily. But yours is an unlisted number, not out there in the public. How did they find it?"

Silver's eyes shot to his, startled as she realized that was true.

"Someone is playing me, Sorley. And it has to be someone close to me or with the authorities. Not many people have that number." She slumped back against the bench, not feeling Sorley's arm around her.

"Someone is. We'll figure it out. But for now, we need to find a way to keep you safe." Sorley's eyes were on her face. "Yes, someone is going to a lot of work to threaten you and yes threaten me. What steps can we take to keep you safe?"

Silver shrugged, not sure where he was heading with his words. All she knew was that she was terrified, not at all what she was normally like.

"Marry me, sweetheart. Marry me and let me keep you safe." Sorley's voice was barely audible, his heart on his face and in his eyes.

Silver froze for a moment before she looked up at him, seeing his emotions and feelings for her. She felt hope for the first time in days.

—

"Do you mean that, Sorley? You're just not asking for nothing??"

"I mean it, Silver. It's likely too early to say, but I love you. I think I loved you from the first moment that I laid eyes on you. I am so afraid for you. I don't want to see you hurt or killed. I don't know that I can prevent but I want to spend all the time that God gives us with you."

Silver hesitated, knowing that once she spoke, life would be different for her.

"I love you too, Sorley. I thought that it was too soon."

"It's not. God has led us to one another. I have prayed over this and have not had Him stop me in any way. Will you?" Sorley waited, hardly breathing as she studied him.

"I will. Sorley? What will people say?"

He shrugged, knowing that their friends and families were expecting it. His own family had been dropping hints. He reached to kiss her before wrapping her into his arms. They sat, silent for the moment, but knowing that they had to make plans at some point.

Chapter 17

Meg stared at her daughter that afternoon. Silver had shown up, Sorley heading for his own parents. She shook her head. She could not have heard her daughter correctly.

"Silver? What did you just say?" Meg's eyes raised to Saul who stood with an arm around his daughter, Seamus beside him.

"I said I need to try on your wedding dress." Silver's beautiful eyes were troubled but also holding hope. "Sorley and I want to get married. We do love each other, Mom."

Saul's arm tightened around Silver's shoulders.

"This is so sudden, love. Are you sure?" Saul had expected this but not so suddenly.

"We are, Dad. It's sudden, I know. We've talked. We are sure about it. He loves me, Dad. He makes me feel safe, cherished, and loved." She turned as she heard a sound from Seamus, finding her brother reaching to hug her. "Seamus?"

"He's the knight in your stories, Silver. We can all see that. Now, what can we do?" Seamus supported his sister, even if he felt it was rushed. He had seen the two of them together. He and Sorley had shared a meal just a couple of days prior and he knew that the man was deeply worried about Silver.

Silver hugged her brother before she turned to her mother to be enveloped in that woman's arms.

"Silver, how soon?" Meg shared a look with Saul, knowing that her daughter was rushing into something but that she would have prayed it through as would have Sorley. God did this sometimes, she knew, her thoughts turning to Andrew and Phoebe, Silas and Madigan, and also Grady and Eineen. All three of those couples had married quickly and were deeply in love with one another.

"Soon, Mom. Sorley has gone to speak with his parents. We'll be looking at a couple of weeks, if possible." Silver sighed, knowing that she also had to speak with Richard and her team members.

"Then, we work with what you have decided. I know that you don't want a huge wedding. You never had. Talk to us about your thoughts and then we'll make plans. I'll call Sari later."

"Thanks, Mom. We do want to work with both families." Silver sighed. "And I have to talk to Richard."

Saul began to laugh, his mirth spilling over to the rest of his family.

"You do at that, love. And he will just say that he told you so."

"He will." Silver paced away, needing a break from her family. She reached for her phone, seeing the message from Sorley. She smiled, needing the reassurance of his love.

Seamus watched his sister, knowing that she would have mixed emotions. He read it correctly, he thought, moving in to stand beside her.

—

"Silver? What can I do?"

Silver shrugged, not sure what she wanted him to do.

"I'm not sure, Seamus. We just want a small wedding. I know the church family will want to be there." She sighed as she felt her phone vibrate again. This time, it was Richard, asking what she had just gone and done. She frowned at him and then up at Seamus. "How did he know?"

"Know what? He asked what?" Seamus reached for her phone, reading her message.

"Does he know what we planned? And how could he?" Silver grabbed her phone back, reaching to call Richard. "Richard? It's Sunday. What's up?"

"Silver? Where are you?" Richard's words were rushed, totally unlike his normally calm demeanour.

"With my family. Why?" Silver's eyes were on her brother who stood listening intently to her side of the conversation.

"Why? Because I received a letter on my door today. It was there when I came home from church. It threatens you directly. Now, what do we do with you?" Richard paced his office, worried about his friend, the other team members pacing around his home. Tate was there, he knew as was Mae, in his kitchen, working to prepare a meal for them. None of them had eaten.

"You did? What does it say? I can head your way."

"No!" Richard's comment was forceful and caused Silver to move the phone from her ear. "Stay where you are. Bill was looking for you as was Lily. They'll head to you. And we will meet today, Silver. We'll head your way. Where's Sorley?"

"Was he threatened too? He was heading for his family." She looked around as she heard the door open. "Scrap that. He and his family are here." She pocketed her phone, cutting off Richard's words, to Seamus' great delight. Mirth brimmed in his eyes as he watched Sorley move towards his sister.

"Silver? What's happening?" Sorley waited for her to speak, hearing the greetings and conversation between their parents. Sean stood nearby, a frown on his face.

"Richard called me. There was a threat on his door today, directed at me. I think you too. He's heading this way."

Thirty minutes later, the house seemed overflowing with people. Richard and the others had arrived as had Lily and Bill. Richard studied the couple in front of him, sensing something had changed between them but not sure just what

"Richard? What did the letter threaten?" Silver reached for Sorley's hand, needing that contact with him.

"That they would find you. And that you would not escape this time, even if it meant your death. And that being with Sorley would not protect either one of you. That's the gist of it. They didn't exactly say how

—

they would find you or what they would do to you. You're too familiar with all this, Silver."

"I know, Richard. I know." Silver drew in a deep breath, her hand raising to brush her hair from her face. She didn't realize that it was her left hand that she had raised, the sparkling emerald ring just placed on it visible to all around her.

"Silver?" Naomi reached for her friend's hand. "What is this?"

That comment dropped into the silence of the living room stopped Silver's hand from moving. Sorley's hand tightened on hers, giving her strength to meet her team mates' eyes. She searched each one, seeing understanding in Timothy's and Naomi's, a question before acceptance in Stephen, and then there was Richard. Richard drew in a deep breath, knowing that Silver and Sorley had taken a step that they were confident in.

"Silver? Sorley?" Richard waited patiently, knowing Silver would speak when she could.

Silver searched his face before nodding.

"We're engaged, Richard. We want to get married soon. We have peace about it."

Richard waited before he reached to hug Silver and then Sorley.

"Okay, then. Congratulations. We'll discuss this letter further with Lily and Bill. Then we want to hear your plans."

—

Chapter 18

Richard walked towards his office building the next day, puzzling at something that he could not quite remember. Silver's news the day before had taken them all off guard but they had to admit that it was expected.

Silver wandered the offices, finding a seat in Richard's. Her notebook hit her knee as her thumb clicked at her pen. Timothy watched her, knowing that she was taking the step that he and Tate were planning. Naomi stood beside him, watching Stephen as he sat beside Silver, not speaking, just letting her know that he was there.

Sitting behind his desk, Richard waited for a moment before he began to pray for his team and the decisions that they were looking at making. He had had a long talk with Abe, asking the questions that he had needed to in order to get a sense of what was ahead for them. He had also looked at their books, seeing the number of tasks on them and knowing that he just wanted to be done with the traveling.

Richard raised his head, his eyes studying each one of his team members. Two now had significant others in their lives, and he was glad for them. He studied the two remaining ones and sighed. It was only a matter of time until they did the same. And then there was him. He was growing as restless as the others, wanting to find that special lady to share his life.

"Richard? Where do we stand for now? How far down are we scheduled?" Stephen spoke up, his eyes on his notepad. He had a good idea of where they stood. He just needed that confirmation.

"About four weeks down for now. And then we have a two-week break. We need that. However if we work hard over the next five weeks, we could switch over to training. I'm not sure if we would be able to do that so soon."

Naomi grinned, holding up a folder, a thick folder at that.

"We can. Richard, I have been working on this for a while, since before Timothy met Tate. I could see it happening. These are ideas and suggestions that we've all had over the past year. I've organized it, reached out to suppliers and gotten quotes, and talked to Abe and his guys. I know that you have as well. There are copies here for each of us. We read them, argue them over and then pray about them. Then we decide. I think that we're on the right track, though."

"Thank you, Naomi. I am sure each of you has your thoughts on this. Let's discuss it and then go home to pray over it. Timothy, that means you pray it over with Tate. Silver?" He waited until she looked up at him. He grinned at her, seeing her discomfort for a moment. "And you get to do the same with Sorley. He'll back you whatever your feelings are."

"He will." Silver was still hesitant about the changes that she and Sorley were planning. "I know that he will. We're just so new as a couple though."

"You are. And you are in danger." Stephen spoke up, having had a talk with Timothy. "We're behind you as well, Silver. If you decide you can't do

—

95

this any more, then we will miss you but wish you the best and pray for you. We pray that you don't. That's a decision you will need to make with him as it does affect him as well."

"Thank you all. Now, for this?" Silver was thinking hard about where the team went. "You're okay with this, Richard?"

"I am, Silver. I am. It's time. I never planned on working out of the area for years. Of course, we will still do security in this area if we are asked and we can. That's what we do."

Silver walked away from the meeting, Naomi beside her. Naomi had driven them to the meeting, needing to speak with Silver. Only she had not found the words that she needed.

"Naomi? Can I ask you something?" Silver's head went back as she looked up at the sky. She then reached to open the car door

"Sure." Naomi didn't start the car, watching Silver instead. "What do you need to ask?"

"I'm not sure. This scares me, what is going on. I can't imagine how it will end. I talked to Bill today. He doesn't have a lot of information to work with. He doesn't even have a name to look at. Emma's trying but she's running into road blocks as well. I hate this. I can feel storms gathering around Sorley and me. I am scared for him. For our team. For our families."

"And you will be. It's part of caring about people." Naomi drove away, watching the small car that followed them. "We have a tail, Silver."

<hr>

"We do?" Silver shifted to look behind her. "They're staying back far enough so that we can't see them. Now where?"

"We lose them." Naomi suddenly spun her wheel, heading back the way that they had just come from, passing the car. Silver's phone was out as she snapped a quick picture of it, hoping to get their license plate as well.

Silver watched as the car did the same before Naomi was off onto another street and then another, ending up at the police department. The two ladies were out of the car and running for the door, ending up at the desk. The desk officer looked up at them and nodded when they asked for either Bill or Lily.

Lily approached them, a frown on her face. She had tried to find Silver earlier that day and had been unsuccessful. Now, here she was in front of her.

"Silver? Naomi? What are you doing here?" She reached for the phone that Silver was handing over to her. "Come on back to my office." She handed over the visitor badges.

"We were followed as we left Richard's. Silver took a photo of the vehicle." Naomi watched Silver, seeing her agitation.

Lily studied the photo and then forwarded it to herself. She then enlarged it and worked to find the plate number. Running it, she drew in a deep breath. This was worse than they had thought.

"Silver? Do you have any idea who could be after you?" Lily's head raised when Silver didn't answer. "Silver? Did you hear me?"

Silver looked up, her hand tightening on her phone.

"No, I don't, Lily." She blinked rapidly, her emotions out there for the other two ladies to see. "Sorley just sent a text message. His house is on fire."

"What!" Lily was on her feet, running for her vehicle even as Silver and Naomi ran for Naomi's.

The ladies headed for Sorley's home, stopping short as they saw the emergency vehicles there. Silver was out of the car, searching for Sorley, her body hitting him before he had even turned to see who was running towards him. Naomi followed even as Lily headed for the fire captain.

"Sorley? You're okay?" Silver's arms tightened around him.

"I am, sweetheart. I am. I just don't understand this." He watched as the fire crew fought to bring the fire in his garage under control and to keep it from spreading to his home. This was one time that he was thankful that his garage was detached.

Chapter 19

Sorley walked his house late that afternoon or early evening, he decided as he squinted at the clock. Silver's hand was tight in his. She had simply stood with him all that time, an arm around him, watching and waiting. He could appreciate her silence, knowing that if she felt the need to speak then she would.

His parents were around, he knew, his father outside with the insurance adjuster. Sorley was hurt, his garage burnt beyond repair. He was thankful that no one was hurt. The building and what was in it could be replaced. His car had been parked on the street, where he had left it, planning on going back out. Only that had not happened. He had been inside the house, setting away the few purchases that he had made. His plans had been to head for Silver. Instead, Silver had found him.

Silver's hand tightened on Sorley's. She wasn't sure if the fire had been accidental or aimed at him. And just why the garage would burn? She was determined to find out. Silver knew that her team had been around and then had scattered. Richard had simply hugged her and told her to call him, if not that night, then in the morning.

Sorley turned at last, standing in his office, his arms wrapping around Silver. They simply stood, not hearing the footsteps heading their way. Shannon and Sean stood there, Saul and Seamus with them. The four men exchanged glances before Shannon spoke.

"Sorley? Son? The adjuster would like to speak with you. Do you have a few moments?"

Sorley nodded, not wanting to leave Silver. He dropped a kiss on her forehead before he walked away, the two younger men with him. Shannon and Saul exchanged glances.

"Silver? What happened? Do you know?" Saul approached his daughter, finding her backing away from him.

"I don't, Dad. I really don't. I was in a meeting. Naomi and I were followed. We were with Lily when Sorley sent his text message. We came right here." Silver was deeply afraid, something now common for her. She was known among her family and friends to be fearless.

"I see. This vehicle? Did you see it?" Shannon was worried about his son, more worried than he cared to admit. He thought that Sorley working in finance would mean that he was safe. He had not realized exactly what his son did until he had sat down with him the previous evening and had a talk. He could understand why Sorley had not told them, wanting to keep them as safe as he could.

"We did, Dad. I took a picture and Lily has it. She was working on it when Sorley's call came in." She paced, not hearing the footsteps sounding through the house. Not that it would have mattered to her. She just wanted this over, and that didn't seem possible at the moment.

Abe Finlay stood there, called in by Richard. He watched Silver carefully before he nodded. *She's in work mode,* he thought, *assessing the situation and trying to determine how best to proceed. I had prayed that this would not happen to any more of my friends. Lord, You are in control. It is as You will that things happen. You do not allow anything that would be apart from that.*

"Silver?" Abe spoke from where he stood near the doorway, seeing as she jerked and then faced him. Shannon stared at him, not knowing who he was but Saul reached to shake his hand.

"Abe?" Silver spun, surprise on her face. "You're here? Don't tell me. Richard called you in, didn't he?"

Abe grinned at the disgruntled tone in her voice.

"He did. He wanted to pick my brain, as he called it. You know what we went through, what our friends and your friends faced. Together, we make a team that is almost unstoppable. We work together, not against one another."

"We do. And Emma's in on the search, isn't she?"

Abe continued to grin, knowing that his wife, Emma, whose business called Trackers could find people and information that no one else seemed able to find, was involved.

"She is. And so is my team. And I hear tell that Don is weighing in. Now, tell me what happened today. Richard had called me before this happened."

"Sorley's garage was torched. We don't know why. It could be related to what we're going through

---

or to an investigation that he's involved in." Silver walked past him, a hand catching at his arm. "Come with me. You too, Dad and Shannon. Let's find Sorley, introduce you, and then see what your plans are that we won't go along with." She smirked as he broke out into laughter. "All the ladies say that as do the men. And just where is Ian planning to fly us to where no one would find us?"

Abe laughed harder before he could sober up enough to explain to the two older men that Ian was one of his team members and always offered that to the ladies in trouble.

Sorley turned as he felt Silver's arm around him, simply wrapping her into a hug. He blinked back tears, his emotions raw from the fire. He coughed slightly from the smoke that still hung in the air. He would need to write a list of what was in the garage, as best he could, and get it to his insurer. At the present time, all he wanted to do was hold Silver and not let her go. Lily had been grim when she approached him not that long before. It had been arson, she informed him, and just who did he tick off so badly or was it related to what he and Silver had gone through? He had shrugged, not sure of that.

"No one should have my name, Lily. Not unless someone has spoken out of turn. I do the investigation, turn it over to the authorities. They verify it and then lay charges if charges are warranted. I am not part of that process or the court process."

"I see. I thought that you would be out there." Lily tapped at her lips with a slim forefinger. "Stay safe, Sorley. I don't want to see either you or Silver hurt."

"Nor do I, Lily. I want to keep her safe. Only, I don't know how to do that. She knows more about that than I do." Sorley rubbed at his head. His headache that had finally left him was back and throbbing in his temples.

"Talk to her. Talk to Richard or any of their team. They can provide that information for you." Lily walked away, not satisfied that she had all the information that she needed. There had been no warning, no letter left, nothing that would help.

Sorley turned at last to face his father, Saul, and Abe. He frowned at Abe.

"Abe? You're here? Why?"

"You bring me here, Sorley. You and Silver." Abe knew Sorley from working on cases. He had not let that fact out, knowing that he couldn't. "I heard from a friend that another friend was in trouble. Emma sent me."

Sorley grinned for a moment, knowing that Emma would have done that.

"Your guys?"

"Still at home. They were deep in training a team in. I freed myself up to come. Listen, we need to get you two out of the open and into the house." Abe could feel the tingling in his neck. "Now!"

The group ran for the house, Abe following, his eyes searching the area. Richard had returned just in

time to see this. He nodded, heading around the house
to search as did the other three of his team.

Chapter 20

Ten days later, Sorley stood in the church hall of their church, an arm around Silver. Silas and Madigan approached them, watching closely before sharing a glance.

"Sorley? Silver?" Madigan reached to hug them.

"We're okay, Madigan." Silver hastened to reassure her friend. They had only had their family and close friends there. Unbeknownst to them, Don and Abe had appeared with their teams, ready to watch out for them.

A week later, Silver moved through Sorley's home, now hers. She was still somewhat uncertain that they had made the right move, as much as in love with her groom as she was. Richard had called her earlier, letting her know that one of Don's men had stepped in for the next couple of weeks, just as a gift for her. He would use her in the office instead, finalizing their plans for transitioned to training. She had been happy to do that even though she was saddened not to be out with the team.

Sorley stood and watched her for a moment before he glanced down at the mail. He sighed. His call to Bill had not been unexpected, he found. Bill had promised to come around that evening, if he could and wasn't intruding.

"Silver, sweetheart?" Sorley hated to disturb the happiness that glowed on his bride's face.

<hr>

Silver turned, sobering as she saw the stern look on his face.

"What did we get, Sorley?"

"This. A letter. And photos from our wedding. At least they weren't from where we escaped to."

"No, that's a relief." She reached for them, a frown on her face. "This is odd, Sorley. They're from inside the church and even down at the reception. I don't remember any strangers being there but there could have been."

"There were no strangers there, love. Just family and friends and ones from the church." He paled. "The church?"

Silver nodded, having already come to that conclusion that someone there was involved. She just didn't know who it was. And that was concerning. If they didn't know who it was, then they could not protect themselves.

Sorley watched her closely before he turned, pulling her with him. He reached for the church photo directory.

"Here. Let's go through this and see if we can figure out anyone. I know that they are not going to jump off the page at us."

Silver sighed, knowing that he was correct. She still reached for it, looking through it. She paused at a few photos, Sorley writing them down to pass on to someone. Only, he didn't know who that someone was.

Richard turned from watching the street as the door opened behind him. Silver stood there, an unreadable look on her face.

"Silver? Welcome home." Richard reached to hug her and then stood back, assessing her.

"Thank you, Richard. We're in the kitchen. Have you eaten yet?"

Richard nodded, knowing that Silver would feed him anyway.

"I have, Silver. Thank you for asking. I'll just have some coffee or tea if you have that."

"We do." Sorley turned from the stove, setting plates on the table. A hand on Silver's shoulder had her sitting while he poured their hot drinks.

Richard watched them closely, seeing the happiness that was evident but also the worry and fear underneath. He knew that they were worried about one another. Only he knew that what he had to say would not relieve that, not at all.

Richard set his mug down, his eyes on it, before he asked if he could pray for them. Sorley nodded, knowing Richard well enough that he would.

"Richard, what have you found out?" Silver was afraid to hear the answer

"Not a lot, Silver. I'm sorry. This is not going very far for you in its resolution. And we all fear that you two marrying will only drive up the stakes."

"We know that they will." Silver shared a look with Sorley. "Here. We got this today. Take copies of it." Silver passed over the letter and the photos.

Richard studied them before he frowned at the couple.

"That's from the church and inside it."

"We know that. We think that it's someone from the church who is involved. We think we have some names. We just don't want to accuse anyone until we know for sure." Sorley shoved across the piece of paper that he had scribbled the names down on.

Richard took it, knowing that Silver would not have put the names down without a reason. He looked down at them, fear growing in his heart. He knew the couples. Most were prominent in town, but one couple was very silent in town. He sighed, knowing that their work had just begun. His phone was out as he sent the names off to Emma.

"Emma will look into them, Silver. She'll contact us with what she has."

"I know that she will. I'm scared, Richard, and I don't scare." Silver felt Sorley's hand tighten on hers.

"We know that you are and that you don't. You can't, not in our line of work." Richard sat back, his mind working at scenarios and solutions. "We don't know who will come after you next, now do we?"

"No, we don't. And if we don't, we can't take precautions." Silver's mind drifted from the conversation between the two men. She rose, heading for the computer, a thought crossing her mind. She searched, not sure what she was looking for before she sat back. She sighed. *No, this is not working. I need to solve this but I don't know how.*

Sorley found her later, pulling her up and then down on his knee as he sat in her chair. He didn't say anything, just held her.

"What did you discover?" Sorley hurt for his bride, wanting this over.

"I don't know that I found anything. How do we investigate this, Sorley? How do we find the ones responsible before they kill one of us?" Silver hugged him, tears on her face that she didn't even try to hide from him.

Chapter 21

Silver was tired. They had had to be away overnight, not by choice but because the person who they had been providing security for had had a medical emergency. They could not leave the man until other security was in place. The whole team was exhausted. Richard assessed each one, his eyes lingering on Silver for a moment. This was wearing them all down, he thought, but particularly Silver and then Timothy. Both wanted to keep their significant others safe but were not sure if they could. Timothy had approached him the day before, asking if he thought that two different parties were involved. It just seemed that there were.

Richard had agreed but had not had a chance to speak with Timothy any further about that. He needed to think it through and then seek counsel on it. This was out of his experience and training.

Sorley turned from the back door, hearing the front door open and close. Silver was home, he thought, moving that way. Silver had not seen him, expecting that he would be in his office. She slumped with fatigue, only wanting a shower and then sleep. Hearing a slight noise, she raised her head, her eyes meeting Sorley's before she threw herself at him.

"Sorley? I thought that you would be at work."

"No, I'm working from home today. I was waiting for you to come home. Go and shower, sweetheart. I'll make something light for you to eat.

Then you can sleep." He kissed her, not wanting to release her but knowing that he had to.

Silver smiled at him and then walked away, heading for the shower and clean clothes. Her smile grew as she saw the clothes already placed for her. She turned to stare at the door. Sorley was spoiling her, she decided, and that was just fine in her books.

Sorley looked up three hours later, needing a break from the investigation that he was deep into. Silver had simply curled up on the couch near him, a soft pink blanket covering her. He frowned as he heard a tap at the door and walked that way. Bill stood there, soberness on his face.

"Bill? You're here?"

"I am. Is Silver here?"

"She's sleeping. They didn't get in until this morning. I would prefer not to wake her up if we can avoid it."

"I think that is okay. We'll talk with her later." Bill sat with a sigh. It had been a long day already.

"What do you have?" Sorley waited, his heart praying for his friend. "You're wearing out, Bill. You're carrying a heavy burden, aren't you?"

"I am. I try not to but it can't be helped. I know that God takes our burdens and bears them for us. But because we are human, we think we need to bear them as well."

"That's so true, Bill. Silver and I have to turn this burden of what we're going through over to God every day. We pray for protection for one another, our friends, our families, and people like you who are investigating. You have our prayers just as we have yours.”

“They are appreciated, Sorley. That they are. I have been looking at those names.” Bill hesitated, not sure how Silver had determined them. “How did she come up with them?”

Sorley shrugged.

“I have no idea. She reads people as it’s part of her employment. That doesn’t shut off when she leaves work. She did say that there was something about them that struck her wrong. She just doesn’t know why. I haven’t known too many people who can do that.”

“She’s good. All of Richard’s team is. God has given them a gift that few have. I know some officers who have that innate ability. Most of the time, it’s something that we learn from experience.”

“She is good. She’s scary that way.” Sorley rose to go and check on Silver, tucking the blanket up higher around her neck. A kiss was dropped on her cheek before he padded away on his thick socks.

Bill looked around as Sorley returned. *He’s burning out,* Bill thought, *and we need to end this. Only I don’t know how we do that. God, it’s in Your hands. Guide us and protect these friends of ours.*

“Bill, where exactly do we stand? I know that you can’t give too much information.”

“No, I can’t but I can tell you what I can. We’re looking at those names. We’re investigating the two men who held you captive. There was another man there we know but we don't know who it was. There was no grow-op in the quarry but there are rumours of one nearby. We don't know and can't confirm who it is.

"Now, as to your garage? That's a puzzle. We picked up some activity on one of your security cameras. It was a youth who did this. He's known on the street and we're looking for him there. He's in hiding and for good reason. Heaven help him if we don't catch him. He not likely will survive.

"As to why? We're hearing various rumours, drugs being the top one." Bill hesitated, not sure how to proceed with what he needed to ask.

Sorley nodded, knowing that was likely the case. He frowned as Bill paused.

"Bill? What is it that you need to ask?"

"I don't know how to ask this. I also don't want to put your investigations at risk or anything like that. With your investigations, have you ever come across anyone who is linked with drugs or has been charged and convicted of that?"

Sorley sat back in his chair, his eyes not moving from Bill. He thought through his cases and nodded.

"There have been. What I can do is give you the names of the investigators involved and have you contact them. There are four cases that I am aware of. All from the area although not our town." He reached for a piece of paper and a pen, scribbling down the names. He slid it across to Bill, his eyes on his friend.

"I pray that this works, Bill. We can't do much more than we are. And I want this over."

"We know that you do. We want it over for you as well." Bill studied the names that he had been given, realizing that he knew them.

"Bill? Silver has had another thought. What if there is more than one party involved? She seems to think that someone is after Richard. She can't explain it."

Bill nodded, knowing that they had had the same thought. Richard had in fact discussed it with them.

"We think that there are, but we have no proof. That's part of our investigation."

Chapter 22

Silver walked slowly through her office building the next day. Richard had called a meeting, to which she had reluctantly agreed to come. She was feeling off, not quite herself. She just didn't know why. A fever had awakened her earlier and taking medications had eased it.

Richard watched his team, studying each one, assessing their strengths, before he nodded. He was ready to stop traveling and now was the time to start implementing their plans.

"Okay, people. Let's pray." Richard waited for his team to pray before he finished their time. His prayer was earnest, seeking, full of praise and ending with his usual "I love you" to God. He shuffled his papers, knowing that when he spoke it would change their group.

"Richard? You wanted to meet?" Stephen had his eyes on Silver, watching her intently, sensing that she wasn't well.

"I did. We need to talk about about where we're heading. I met again with Abe and this is the decision that we have come to. You have been part of it. You know what he trains in. He had suggestions for us, based on our experience and personal interests, as to where we start training. There is a need for what we can offer. We would work with him to train, offering to follow up or lead the teams one after the other."

"I never thought of that." Silver leaned forward, squinting for a moment. "That makes sense. Now, when do we start?"

"We're done travelling as of now. I have put off the assignments to someone else. Don was glad to pick up most of them for us as they were only short day-long ones. Now, we meet every day to plan. I have someone working on our website to change it. Abe has names that he will send over to us. Silver, your expertise is investigating these teams. That stays with you and what your training is. Naomi, your expertise is in finding safe houses. That stays with you. Timothy, your expertise is vehicles. Stephen, your expertise is first aid. Mine will be how to coordinate it all."

They worked away for a few hours, sorting out the nitty-gritty parts of it as Stephen phrased it. He kept his eye on Silver, rising at last to crouch down beside her.

"Silver? You're not feeling great."

Silver slowly turned her head, vertigo hitting for a moment.

"No, I'm not, Stephen. I had a fever this morning. Right now, I'm feeling really dizzy." Her eyes closed as she collapsed, Stephen catching her before she hit the floor.

The others were on their feet, running after Stephen, heading for the company vehicle. Richard separated from them, heading for his own car, knowing that he had to reach out to Sorley.

Sorley rose from his office desk, hearing Richard's voice. He walked through to the reception area, finding Richard heading his way. His head began to shake as he saw the grim look on Richard's face.

"Sorley? I need you to pack up what you've been working on. Silver collapsed a few minutes ago. The team is taking her to the hospital. Are you at a point where you can walk away?"

Sorley stared at him and then nodded, back in his office to clean up what he had been working on. His heart sank as he thought of Silver and prayed for her. He didn't think that she had been feeling well that morning but she had just shrugged off his concern.

"Richard? What can you tell me?" Sorley stared out of the side window, not seeing the passing scenery. All of his thoughts were on his bride.

"Silver told Stephen that she had had a fever early this morning and then dizziness. She collapsed as she told us that." Richard parked near the Emergency Entrance. "Come, let's get you inside. The waiting room, I think Sorley for now."

Sorley nodded, wanting to be with Silver but knowing that he had to let the physicians assess her and start her treatment. The team moved around him. He looked up as he felt an arm around his shoulders. Sean was there, called in by Richard.

"Sean? You're here?"

"I am. Richard called me. Seamus is on his way. Apparently our parents are away somewhere together today. I had to leave a voice mail with Dad." Sean watched his brother, afraid to ask. "What happened?"

"I don't know. Richard said that Silver collapsed as they finished a meeting. I don't know much more than that. I didn't think that she was feeling very well this morning but she shrugged me off."

"She does that, Sorley. She does that. She doesn't want you to worry about her. And you are. Hiding that doesn't help." Sean was frustrated with his sister-in-law.

It seemed as if days had passed before Sorley was on his feet, heading back to the exam rooms, the nurse pointing him to one. It had in reality only been about an hour if that. He hesitated as he entered the room, his eyes searching for Silver and finding her. He frowned at the IV lines running to her arms, the oxygen mask, the heart monitor and the other equipment sitting around. He didn't realize that it was so severe.

The physician appeared at his side, reaching to assess Silver's vitals before he wrote in a chart. The chart was closed and set to one side as the physician then assessed Sorley.

"Sorley? What can you tell me?"

Sorley jumped at the voice and then shrugged.

"Not a lot. Stephen could probably tell you more about what happened. She wasn't feeling well this morning, I don't think. She was hiding it, just so I didn't worry."

"And you did." The physician nodded. "Okay, so for what is going on? Right now we're running blood work. She's had imaging. I can't tell you exactly what is going on. She has a fever. Stephen mentioned that she felt dizzy. We're not looking at something benign, however, something like a flu or cold. This doesn't fit with that."

"What are you saying then, doctor? What is wrong?" Sorley grew more scared for his bride. If it wasn't something benign or simple then it was much worse.

"You have been well? No symptoms?"

Sorley shook his head.

"No. I'm okay. But what is it with her?" Sorley drew in a deep breath. "What are you not saying, doctor? Do you suspect drugs, poisoning, or a virus that you don't about?"

The physician nodded. Sorley had gone right to the centre of his thoughts

"That we are, Sorley. I'm sorry that I don't have answers for you. I have spoken with Bill Buckley, and he will be around. He indicated that he expected something like this. I don't understand why."

"Why? Because someone has been after us. We don't know why or we would find them and stop them. I just want this over."

Chapter 23

Sorley paced the parking lot of the hospital, Richard, Timothy, and Stephen side by side with him. His and Silver's brothers were with their parents, waiting inside for news. He had had to get out into the fresh air, even though it was now night and the moon and stars were playing hide-and-seek with the scudding clouds. It was a warm night and Sorley wiped at the sweat gathering on his brow. He prayed for his bride, begging God to spare her life.

Seamus shared a look with Sean before he shook his head. There had not been a lot of word yet. The last update had been that Silver was holding her own. They just didn't know what had happened. Naomi sat nearby, her eyes closed as she prayed for her friend. Silas and Madigan had been there but had had to leave.

Sorley stopped abruptly, his face lifting to the sky. His eyes closed as he fought back tears. He felt hands on his shoulders and heard the prayers for him and Silver, even though his concentration didn't let him hear the words. He appreciated that. He just didn't know where he went from there.

Shannon approached, his eyes worried for his son. He stood for a moment, watching his son. *When did he grow up, Lord? It seems as if just yesterday that I was holding a newborn and then watching him grow into the man he is today. Protect my son, Lord, my oldest. Heal his lady. But prepare us if it is Your will that she goes home. That would hurt but You would heal our hearts.*

Sorley turned once more to walk back to the hospital, finding his father waiting for him. Shannon simply held his son as he wept, his own tears on his face. *He shouldn't be facing this, Lord, not at all. He's too young for this. Please bring the people involved to the authorities and to justice.*

A nurse was looking for Sorley, beckoning him to follow her as he entered. He drew in a deep breath, fearing to go to Silver but knowing that he would be in no other place. His footsteps slowed as he approached the stretcher, his eyes on the bags hanging from the pole attached to the stretcher. His eyes dropped to his bride and a hand reached out for hers.

Silver moved restlessly, her eyes flickering open and closed. She could hear someone speaking to her, asking her to wake up. She was just too tired to respond. She slept, the life-saving fluids dripping down into her hand.

"Sorley?" The physician was back, a chart in his hands. "We've found what it was."

"You did? And?" Sorry didn't look around, not wanting to take his eyes off his bride.

"We did. It was a poison. Bill said that they were trying to track down where she was poisoned."

"And that will be hard. She's all over the place. Although yesterday she spent most of the day at the office with her team."

"Her team?" The physician was puzzled.

"She's on a security team. They have been away at times but if it's been in the last day or so, she's been at home. Where did she get it?"

"Her car." Bill spoke from behind him, causing him to spin. "We've tracked it to inside her car, spread on her gear shift."

"Her gear shift? They accessed her car?" Sorley spun, a hand reaching out to catch at the stretcher bedrail.

"They did. We just don't know when. Talk to me, Sorley. Tell me about her day." Bill drew him away from the stretcher to a corner where they could speak.

"She was in the office until about three, I think. Then, she went shopping for groceries. And I think that she went to the pharmacy and the florist. I'm sorry. I really don't know exactly."

"That's okay. We'll speak with staff in the stores there to see if they were aware of anything." Bill watched Sorley, trying to assess if there was anything else. "Sorley, do we have permission to go through your home?"

Sorley drew in a deep breath and nodded, his eyes on Silver. He didn't want to leave her but he would if necessary.

"You can." He turned to walk from the room, stopping as Bill's hand rested on his arm. "Bill?"

"Your father or brother? They have keys to your home?" Bill was trying to find someone who had access to Sorley's home without Sorley being forced to leave Silver.

"Both do. Sean will go. You have permission to search my home and take anything that you suspect." Sorley's eyes bored into Bill's. "I didn't do this, Bill. I couldn't. I just don't know who did. Find them." He walked away, back to his bride, a hand out to rest on her hair.

Bill watched him for a moment, knowing that he would be a suspect until he was proven innocent. And innocent he was, of that Bill was certain.

Sean stood as Bill motioned him over.

"Bill?" His worried look shot back towards the door and then to Bill.

"I need to search Sorley's home. He tells me that you have a key to it."

"I do, but I don't understand why." Sean slipped into the passenger's seat, fastening his seatbelt before Bill drove away.

"Silver was poisoned and we don't know how or when. We need to go through their home."

Sean paled at that thought before his mind was racing.

"Bill, before you do, please obtain a warrant. Take the legal route on this. I know that Sorley had given his permission, but that could be used against him."

Bill nodded, having already reached out to Lily. He was praying that they found nothing in the house.

He had had a friend go through being the suspect in his wife's near death and he didn't want to go through that again.

Lily was waiting for him, warrants in hand, as well as a crime scene tech team standing on the porch. Sean paled even more as he walked towards them, unlocking the door, and turning off the security system. He then turned and walked away, to lean against a tree, his eyes glued to the house. *Please, Lord, don't let them find anything. Sorley doesn't need this, not when Silver is so sick.*

Chapter 24

Bill walked through the house, his eyes searching for anything that stood out. Only, nothing stood out. The house was tidy and clean, everything in its place. That was what he had expected. He turned as Lily approached.

"Lily?"

"We didn't find anything, Bill. Not one thing. And it isn't as if the house was cleaned up to hide anything. It's not them."

"No, it's not. And Sorley did say that Silver hasn't been at her own place for a few days. We'll look there, just in case."

Lily nodded, a frown on her face.

"If it's in her car, who did it? I have someone tracking her steps yesterday. She really didn't go to many places."

"And we're assuming that this was done yesterday. Did the physician say if it is a fast-acting one?" Bill walked out of the house and towards Sean.

"No, I don't know that he did. The consensus seems to be that it was a fast-acting one."

"Bill?" Sean straightened up, hope on his face.

"Nothing, Sean. You can lock up." Bill watched as Sean did so before they were back in the car, heading for the hospital.

———

Lily had reached out to Seamus, asking him to meet her at Silver's. She just prayed that there was nothing there.

Seamus watched from the doorway as Lily and the team walked through the house, praying as well that there was nothing there. He didn't think that they would but he just wasn't sure. He breathed a sigh of relief as Lily walked towards him, shaking her head.

"Her house is clear, Seamus. She hasn't been here in the last few days, I don't think."

"Not that I know of. If you're done. I'll lock up and then head back to the hospital."

Lily watched as Seamus drove away, her thoughts troubled. Something was missing here and she had no idea what. She sighed as she turned for her car, stopping as a woman appeared in front of her. She frowned.

"Sandy? What are you doing here?" Lily reached to draw Sandy to her vehicle.

"Lily? Silver? She's in danger. Here. Take this." Sandy shoved a package at her and was gone before Lily could react.

Lily studied the package before she dropped ii on the car seat. She drove away, heading for the office, her eyes glancing at the package every once in a while. She parked and then reached for the package, heading for the crime lab.

"Sid? Do you have a moment?" Lily held up the package. "I need you to go over this for me."

"What do you have?" Sid approached her, snapping gloves on as he did so.

"I was handed this. I need you to go over it before I look through it." Lily waited patiently for him to finished. She looked down into the box, a frown at what it contained.

"This is strange, Lily." Sid stared at the box and then at her.

"It is, Sid." Lily reached for the contents, setting them down on the table. "A thumb drive. Photos of Sorley and Silver." She used a pen to sort through the photos, realizing that they were mostly of Silver. "This is strange, Sid. I don't see anything odd."

Sid shook his head.

"It is strange, Lily. There are hardly any of Sorley. Silver? Who has been following her this closely? These are all time stamped as well."

Lily nodded, having noted that.

"They are. All off from yesterday." Lily quickly sorted them by the time stamp. "This confirms what Sorley told Bill. Other than the stop for gas." Lily looked up, a frown on her face. "Sid? There's something off about that pump." She was away, Sid staring after her before he turned to sort the items into evidence bags and then set them aside.

Lily headed for the gas station, asking for their video surveillance from the previous day. She stared at it, her heart falling as she saw what had happened. Asking for a copy of it, she tucked the thumb drive into an evidence bag and then headed for the office. She needed to look back through it, print off photos, and then find Bill.

Bill turned as he heard rapid footsteps, turning to find Lily nearing him,

"Lily?" He reached for the folder that she was thrusting at him. "What's this?"

"I found out where Silver was poisoned. At the gas station. Sandy gave me a package that contained time-stamped photos of Silver from yesterday. Sorley was almost right. He just didn't say that she went to the gas station."

"The gas station? It was there? You have proof? Of course, you do. And this is it?" Bill held up the folder.

"It is. I printed off stills for you to look at. I couldn't get a good look at the man's face but he was definitely tampering with the hose. And then he hangs around, watches Silver, and then cleans off the pump when she's done. I've sent Sid to see what he can find, but we're not hopeful that he can find much. Too many people had been through there."

"That's true. And he could say it wasn't him, even though we have proof." Bill studied the photo. "Sid is working on these?"

"He is. He's setting aside something else that he's waiting for results on and doing this. He wants it over. Silver has been good to his family over the years. He won't say what but knowing Silver, she's gone out of her way to help him."

"She does that, as do all of Richard's team. They are a real support in our town, without asking for anything. All we can do is pray for protection for them. I don't think that this will end with Silver."

"It never does. And how is she?" Lily turned towards the waiting room, not seeing any of the family.

"They moved her to a floor. They were able to find an antidote and it's working. She's not totally awake yet but she is rousing."

"That's good. I'm off and back to the office before I get called out somewhere else." Lily sighed as her phone chimed. Reading the test, she grumbled for a bit. "And I just got called. Catch me later, Bill."

———

Chapter 25

Sorley pulled up a chair and sank into it, his eyes sliding closed. He was exhausted, his emotions raw. He didn't look up as he heard footsteps approaching him and then coming to a stop. He waited before he cracked open his eyes. Andrew stood there, watching him.

"Andrew? You're here?"

"I am. Just as a friend, Sorley. Bill's working the case." He looked towards Silver. "How is she?"

"Improving. Thank God that they found the antidote so quickly. I haven't heard just what poison it was and I'm not sure that I want to know." Sorley felt as if he was hiding his head in the sand and could not do anything other than that.

"I know, Sorley. It's hard to have someone go through this. I've a friend whose now wife was poisoned and kept being poisoned. She did almost die. I'll put you in touch with Murphy and Adriel. They'll be glad to talk it over with you and Silver. Silver does know them."

"She does? Who doesn't she know?" Sorley sighed even as Andrew laughed at him.

"She does know a lot of people, given her work and how friendly she is. She does seem to be reserved but she does accrue friends."

———

"She does." Sorley was on his feet, his hand on Silver's face as she began to toss and turn. His touch eased her agitation and she slept once more.

Andrew spent some time with Sorley, praying with him before he walked away. He was unsettled in doing so, knowing that Sorley and Silver were still in danger. They just didn't know who was after them.

Carrying Silver into their home the next day, Sorley stared at her beloved face. It was whiter than he liked and her eyes were closed. He set her on her feet before he wrapped a blanket around her and then shoved her gently to the couch. A pillow went under her head. Silver gave a sigh of relief. She was home but not well enough to appreciate it.

Richard walked through the house behind Sorley, searching for anything off. He didn't find anything and knew that the other three team members were searching outside. He wasn't content with what he had been told. *Sure,* he thought, *someone could have tampered with the pump as in the photos. I need to start picking up more on the investigation and reaching out to my resources.*

Sorley paused and turned to watch Silver. She was sleeping again, something that she would be doing a lot of over the next few days. He had already been warned about that.

Richard turned, looking past Sorley towards the two families who had gathered there. They wanted to be there for their children, not sure yet what had happened. He could not explain it to them. He wasn't sure if he ever would be able to do that.

———

"Sorley?" Sari moved to hug her son, standing with her hands on his arms. "What can we do for you?"

Sorley shrugged.

"I don't know, Mom. I really don't." He turned, staggering for a moment, his fatigue hitting him hard.

Seamus and Sean were there to catch him, hands on his arms to guide him to a chair in the living room. He sat, his head hanging down, fatigue washing over him in waves. His head then went back and he slept. Sari moved in to cover him with a blanket, a hand resting on his head as she prayed for healing for both of the children as they termed them.

Meg hesitated before she moved around the kitchen, knowing that she had to prepare a meal but uncertain that the food stuffs were okay to use.

"Richard? What about the food stuffs? Could they be tampered with?"

"It is possible, Meg. How be we just order something? I know Ev will have food for us." Richard walked away, looking for one of his team to send them, finding that Stephen and Naomi had already left.

Timothy stood near him, searching the area. He was uncomfortable to say the least.

"Someone is out there. And they are not here for the health of Silver and Sorley."

"There is. And you are right." Richard paced the yard, searching for whatever had been placed. And things would be there, of that he was certain. "There, Timothy. Someone has been out here. We'll find cameras more than likely."

"As long as that is all it is. I'm just afraid that something else will be tampered with and neither one will get to medical help in time." Timothy bent over, moving the plants aside to study the camera. "We need to move them somewhere, Richard."

"We do, and it's difficult when they're newlyweds. They need their privacy." Richard rubbed at the back of his neck. "There's the apartment in the office building. We can use that for them. We just need to convince them that they need to."

"Silver will go, I would suspect. She's too savvy not to be aware that needs to be done." Timothy turned as he heard a noise, running towards the back of the yard, Richard on his heels. He leapt towards the form there, taking down the man who had turned to run.

Richard reached to help pull the man to his feet, a frown once more on his face. Dugan Lowe stood there, a sheepish look on his face.

"Dugan? What are you doing here?" Richard reached for his phone, calling in Bill. "This is private property."

"I know. I just worry about Sorley. He's in trouble. I want to help." Dugan was a man who lived on the rough side of the town. He was a kindly man who had been through many troubles in his life.

"What do you know, Dugan? What can you tell us?" Timothy spoke kindly to the man.

Dugan's mouth opened to respond before his body jerked and he collapsed facedown on the ground. A red stain grew on his back. Timothy and Richard dropped as well, eyes searching for the assailant. Timothy's phone was out, calling for aid. Richard reached for Dugan's wrist, his head dropping as he realized that it was too late and that they would never know what Dugan had to tell them.

Chapter 26

Blue and red emergency lights lit up the darkening sky. Men and women officers milled around, joined by teams of paramedics and the fire department. Bill shut his car door, locking it, his eyes on the house. *This is not what they need, Lord. They need peace and quiet and aren't getting it. Please, Lord, could we just have that for a day or two? It's not too much to ask, I don't think. I know that You have them in the hollow of Your hands and want only the best for them. Protect them, please.*

Richard waited for him on the city sidewalk, a closed look on his face. This was not what they had needed in the investigation. He could only pray that Dugan had evidence somewhere and that it was still there. He just didn't think that it would be.

"Bill? What can you tell me to help protect these two?"

Bill shrugged, not sure what he could say. That had shown tonight when Dugan was killed. They were searching but given the dark moving in, it meant that they would be back the next day.

"I'm not sure what we can do to protect them. Whoever is behind this has shown that." Bill walked towards the house. "Are they up?"

"Sorley is. He's tucked Silver into bed. She was awake for a bit but didn't stay awake."

Bill nodded, knowing that would be par for the course over the next few days.

"How does that affect your team?"

Richard sighed, knowing that it would.

"It will. But we'll manage. Both Don and Abe have offered some of their team. We're working through setting up training, picking up where Abe doesn't."

"You are? That sounds much better for you. Your team is starting to settle down. They won't want to travel. Their character is that their families will come first and if necessary, they'll find alternate employment."

"They will and I don't want to see that. I'm getting tired of travelling as well. The last one? It was really brutal and took a lot from us." Richard paused on the porch, his eyes on the front door. "It's been coming for a while. Timothy has been pushing for it since before he met Tate."

"I know. He's vented to me, in a good way, just brainstorming more or less." Bill headed into the house and then through it, the backyard his destination.

Seamus and Sean stood shoulder to shoulder in front of Richard, stern looks on their faces. Their parents had headed home. Richard's team had as well, just asking that he call them to come back if they were needed. The two brothers had refused to leave, wanting to be there but not sure what they could do.

"Richard, what can we do?" Sean spoke up at last.

"I really don't know, Sean. Bill's out there investigating. I need to leave soon. I have a long day tomorrow."

"We're staying. We've booked off tomorrow and our bosses are in agreement. We'll be here for whatever they need. Our Moms will be here too for a while." Seamus walked away, his emotions raw for a moment.

Richard finally walked away, heading for his home. He had not spoken with Sorley, who had already retired. He would speak with him on the next day, when he got a moment.

The next morning, Silver awoke, surprised to find herself in bed and not in the hospital. She shoved herself up, wondering at how weak she felt. Reaching for clean clothes, she showered, feeling refreshed before heading for the kitchen. She had to drag her hand along the wall just to keep her balance.

Sorley turned as he sensed Silver behind him, simply reaching to draw her into his arms. He hugged her tightly, not wanting to let her go. Bill had been around with Lily and informed him where the investigation stood. He had been shocked to learn of Dugan's death, familiar with the man who spent time near his business office.

"Sorley? Where is everyone?" Silver moved away from him, reaching for a bottle of juice and then headed for the living room. She paced that room, knowing that she was in danger and not sure what she could do to protect both herself and Sorley.

"They've gone home. I sent Sean and Seamus home not too long ago. Richard has been around this morning and will be back later." Sorley walked towards her to wrap her into his arms. "We need to talk, sweetheart."

"I know that we do. What happened to me?" Silver leaned against him, content to be held, not feeling strong enough to stay on her own feet.

"You were poisoned and collapsed two days ago at work. Lily tracked it down to the gas station and a pump handle."

"The gas station?" Silver's brow furrowed. "I did stop there. I didn't see anything out of the ordinary and I was watching."

"Apparently, the handle was tampered with before you arrived and then cleaned after you left. You were being monitored, sweetheart."

"I don't see how that could happen. How did they know which pump I would use?"

"That we don't know. Lily's working on that." Sorley had managed to get Silver sitting down. "That's not all. Dugan Lowe was out back, talking to Timothy and Richard. He was shot and killed."

"Who?"

"Dugan. He is someone who I know from around my office. He was worried about us and had information that he didn't have time to pass on." Sorley's arms tightened on her. "I wish he had. Maybe that would have ended this today."

———

"No, I don't think that it would have." Silver yawned, snuggling down against him. "Is it over yet?"

"No, it's not. Richard received a package containing photos of you from the day you collapsed. Someone was following you everywhere, except to the gas station. That makes us wonder why."

"Because whoever it was that tampered with the handle would have been in the pictures. Did they get the surveillance tape from there?"

"I have no idea. I would suspect so as Lily had information that she only shared with Bill." Sorley's head rested against hers.

"No, they can't tell us. I wonder if Emma could get a copy. I need to reach out to her." Silver dozed off, her head on Sorley's shoulder. He was content to sit there for now but he did have work waiting that he needed to get to.

Sorley rose at last, walking away to his office, not content that he had to but knowing that he had no choice.

God? Is this where You step in? Step in to heal and protect? I know that's what You promise. I am clinging to those promises. I am standing fast on them. And I know that You never fail, never break any of Your promises. For that, I praise You, Lord.

Chapter 27

Two days later, Silver looked up from her desk in the office building. She had simply walked in and gone to work, her eyes on the folders set on it. She felt as if she was running from behind trying to catch up.

Richard had noticed her office lights on as he approached the building. A conference call had taken his attention before he could approach her. He stood at last, heading for her office, hearing conversation from the other offices. His team was together once more, each working through the process of changing their focus to training from actually being the security team itself. He paused in Silver's doorway, watching her for a moment. *She's stressed,* he thought. *Stressed and worried. And she should still be at home on sick leave but is refusing to do that. And I can't force her. I don't have the heart to do that. She's been through enough, and it's far from over for her and Sorley. She's a special lady, Lord, and the first of us to step out away from her friends and family and take on a life mate. We're happy for her but also so worried.*

Silver looked up as Richard took a seat in front of her desk, sitting back and dropping the pen to the desktop.

"Richard?"

"How are you, Silver? And don't tell me that you're fine. I know better. We've been through too much together as a team."

Silver nodded, knowing that he was correct.

"I'm getting there. It will take time, I've been told, to get back to full strength. I reached out to Murphy's Adriel and talked with her. She was poisoned at one point as well."

"She was? I hadn't heard that. She'll have good ideas for how to take care of yourself." He watched her intently, knowing that there was more on her mind.

"Sorley talked to me yesterday. He told me about Dugan."

"Dugan. Yes. Now, that's an odd situation. He didn't seem to want to come to the house. Unfortunately, we didn't get much of a chance to speak with him before he died."

"That's so sad, Richard. Now, how do we find out what he knew?" Silver and Sorley had tried to come up with a plan but hadn't been able to.

"Timothy's been working that line, trying to find out. He's talking with Bill as well, keeping in the loop as much as he can."

"Good. I can reach out to contacts in the downtown area around Sorley's office. He can ask as well and is ready to do that. He's been working from home right now and is planning on heading back down there next week. He has asked if we could do a sweep of his office inside and out."

"That goes without saying, Silver. Stephen is already doing the outside every day. He'll do the inside or one of us will. It's better that it's not you."

"That's what we thought. So we'll leave sit to you until we feel a need to bring in the authorities. And I pray that we never in that position."

"We are too but be prepared for it." Richard nodded towards her desk. "How it is going working on transitioning?"

"It's hard work, Richard. I'm scared to do this seeing as it's so different from what we do. I'm not sure that I can teach."

"You can teach, Silver. You do it all the time when we're away. You do that in a way that isn't looking down on whoever it is that you are speaking with. You teach us how to follow a lead, looking for the least obvious thing to focus on."

"I do, don't I?" Silver's face lit up. "I never thought of that, you know." Silver was happy, knowing that she was where she was useful and wanted. She had feared that she would not fit in with the direction that Richard was taking the team and she would need to leave it, leaving her friends behind.

"You were worried, Silver. Don't be. You have talents and experience that enrich our team, just as the rest do. We have worked together for years, in situations where we have had to learn to trust one another in ways that other businesses don't."

"That's true, Richard." Silver's voice died away for a moment. "Have you thought at all about whether someone is after you and using us to get to you?"

"I have. I've talked to Abe, who faced that very fact. He's given some good advice." Richard stood, his eyes on the window behind Silver. "We're packing it in soon, Silver. One of us will follow you home." He walked away as her mouth opened to say that wasn't necessary before she snapped it closed.

Sorley stood where his garage had. He was disappointed to have to wait to rebuild it but that was how it worked. He didn't turn as he heard footsteps behind him. When no one spoke, he turned cautiously, frowning at the man standing behind him.

"I'm sorry. You're on private property."

"I know that I am. I have a message for you." The man simply stared back at Sorley, the expression on his face not changing.

"I don't know you. Why would you have a message for me?" Sorley stepped backwards, praying that he didn't stumble over any of the debris that remained.

"My boss sent me." The man moved closer to Sorley, a hand out, a knife ripping across Sorley's abdomen before the man turned and casually walked away, leaving Sorley crumbled in the ashes of his garage, blood streaming from the wound across his abdomen.

Silver unlocked the front door, heading inside and kicking off her shoes. Sorley was home, she knew from the car in the driveway. She just couldn't find him in the house. She walked through to the bedroom, changing in more casual clothes before she heard her name being shouted from outside.

———

Timothy had pulled to a stop at the curb, out of his car, following Silver to her door and then walking around the house. He paused, a frown on his face, as he studied the debris from the garage. Something was off there but what it was, he just wasn't sure. As he walked closer, his steps slowed before he was running towards the debris. He was on his knees, hands reaching for Sorley. He stopped in shock as he saw the wound. His phone was out as he called for help. Timothy then turned to shout for Silver.

Silver ran towards him, her bare feet hitting hard on the cement driveway. She slid to a stop, horror on her face as her hands stopped her scream.

"Timothy?"

"I need towels, Silver. We need to try and control the bleeding until the paramedics get here."

Silver was running for the laundry room, grabbing the first towels that she could find, clean ones that were waiting to be taken to linen closet. She was back beside Timothy, reaching to try and help staunch the flow of blood. She glanced at her groom, praying desperately that he would survive.

Chapter 28

Bill strode through the doors of the ambulance bay. His thoughts were troubled. He had been on the scene of a hit-and-run death when the call had come in. He grew a deep breath. Bill just didn't know how much more this couple could take. Sorlry being stabbed was not what he had wanted to hear.

The physician looked around from the desk where he stood, holding up a finger for Bill to wait. He walked towards him after a few moments, pointing to a room.

"In there, Bill. You'll need to see Sorley. We're working on getting him into surgery. And yes, Silver has been back." The physician stopped at Sorley's bedside, reaching to assess him.

"How bad is it?" Bill grimaced at the sight of blood.

"Bad enough. He seems to have been moving back from the knife. This was intentional, Bill. Find whoever it was that did this. He may not survive another attack." The physician looked around. "And I understand that it was his wife who we treated for a poisoning only a couple of days ago."

"It was. She's recovering but doesn't need this. They have only been married for a couple of weeks."

"Only that long? They don't need this." He walked away, leaving Bill staring at Sorley.

———

Silver was distraught. No amount of comforting could calm her down. This was not like her, but Richard, who stood near her, knew that her own health was playing into how she felt. It was also the uncertainty of who it was that was driving her to doubt what was going on.

Timothy, Stephen, and Naomi paced inside and then outside, worried about their friend. This was not how they had planned to end their day. But being not being here was not an option. They supported their friend and team member in everything. Setting aside their own plans for a few hours didn't matter. Timothy knew that Tate was here, inside with Silver. The ladies had become fast friends and Tate would be nowhere else.

Saul and Meg sat on either side of their daughter, needing to be there for her but not knowing exactly what to do. They exchanged glances over her head. Seamus had been there, anger emanating from him before he stalked off to find someone, whoever it was that he could find first. Sean was the first one he met, the two brothers staring at each other before they turned as one and headed outside, knowing that they had seen Richard out there and needing to know what had happened.

Richard had been stunned when Timothy called him. He had just sat down for a meal with Don, who had appeared that afternoon, simply to be there for his long-time friend. Both men had risen, their meal in the restaurant forgotten, money handed to their server before they were running for their vehicles. Hearing Sean's voice calling to him, Richard's eyes had closed for a moment. Don had turned to watch the younger men, seeing the fear and anger in them.

"Richard? What do you know?" Sean's voice held despair.

"Not a lot, Sean, I'm sorry. Timothy found him, brought Silver in, and then called me." Richard's voice held compassion.

"That's what we were told. We were just hoping that you knew more." Seamus paced away from them, circling the parking lot many times. He didn't see Stephen pacing with him, watchful as always, knowing that one of the families could very well be a target just to get to either Sorley or Silver.

Silver rose at last, heading for the exam rooms. She needed to see Sorley, to know that he was still alive. The nurse drew her forward, an arm around her.

"We're getting ready to take him to surgery. They'll be coming for him within five minutes. Stay with him, Silver, until then."

Silver nodded and headed for Sorley. Her hand was on his and the other hand on his face. She prayed for her groom, desperate to know that he would live but also knowing that she had to be ready to let him go. She wasn't ready to do that, not yet.

She stepped back as his stretcher was wheeled away, feeling an arm around her drawing her away and then to an elevator. Saul had appeared, ready to move his daughter to the surgical waiting room, having been warned that Sorley had been taken to surgery and that it would be a while.

———

Silver could never say how much time passed afterwards. She was numb, in shock, and terrified. She couldn't even draw on her training to help her. This was personal, far too personal, and far too frightening for her. Richard and the rest of her team waited with her, moving in and out of the room, ever watchful. Bill had been around, speaking with Timothy, eyeing Silver and then leaving.

Bill headed for Sorley's home, finding Lily still there. They spoke for a while before Bill drove away. He headed for his office, fatigue dragging at him. He squinted at the clock on his computer and sighed. He needed to head for home but he had that report he needed to complete. Rising at last, he stretched, his thoughts turning to Silver and Sorley. *Where did they go with the investigation,* he wondered? *What lead were they lacking that would solve this?* He turned out his office light, locked the door and walked away.

As Bill drove away towards his home, he didn't see the man watching him, then looking down at his hands. The man ran towards the front door of the building, dropping an envelope on the desk when the officer's back was turned and then disappearing. The officer reached for the envelope, stared at it and the door, and then set it aside to give to Bill in the morning.

Silver's head raised at last. She was on her feet, heading for the surgeon, who simply swung around and took her to Sorley. He was still under the effects of the anesthesia but he had survived. They had been able to suture the incision.

"How bad, Doctor?" Silver was afraid to ask.

"He's fortunate, Silver. It wasn't as deep as we thought. There were no internal injuries that we could see. We've sutured the wound closed. He'll sleep for a while. We'll let you in here for now. Then you'll have to leave."

Silver nodded, her attention on Sorley. Sorrow filled her as she studied his pale face. This should not have happened. She just wished that she knew who it was that had done it. She would go after them with everything that was within her. *God, please heal my guy. I can't live without him. Please, Lord, help them to find whoever it was.*

Chapter 29

Silver walked through the downtown area the next morning, heading for Sorley's office. He had been awake, worried about work that he needed to do. Naomi walked with her, not wanting her on her own. Hesitating at the office door, Silver unlocked it and turned off the security system. She hesitated before she moved to the office, turning on the lights and then moving to his desk. His secretary had been in the day before, sorting through what was needed. Silver made a note to thank her.

Naomi waited in the reception area, watchful and listening. She could hear Silver moving around before Silver walked back towards her.

"I'm ready to go, Naomi. I'll need to drop this off at home and lock it away. Sorley will want to be at it right away and he can't."

"No, he can't. Lock up then, Silver, and we'll head that way."

Silver stared at her home, not moving to get out of Naomi's car. She was afraid, she decided, afraid to go into her house. It wasn't that Dugan was killed at the back of their yard. It was that Sorley had been attacked and left for dead here. She didn't know if she could live there any more. That was a discussion she would need to have with Sorley when he was better.

"Silver? Let me pray with you before we go in. I understand that it can be hard for you."

Silver headed for the door. She was ready to go home and stay there. She had spoken with Richard and asked for some time. He had been expecting it, he said. He wanted her to be well and taking the time now would be necessary. He would touch base with her later in the week.

Silver walked through her home, not feeling safe there any more. Naomi had walked through for her and then headed for the outdoors. Silver headed for the safe, locking away the paperwork, and then hesitating. She turned, a frown on her face. Nothing was out of order but she felt uneasy. Heading for the door, she set the security system, locked the door and headed for Naomi.

"You okay?" Naomi studied her friend.

"No, I'm not, Naomi. Something is off and I don't know what it is. I can't explain it. Just a feeling that I have. It's like there's this huge rock balancing on a cliff over our heads and the slightest touch will topple it over and down on us."

"That's a good analogy. It's what it's like." Naomi watched the roads around her, seeing a car tailing them. "We have a tail again. I think it's the same car."

Silver shifted to stare out of the window.

"It is. Let me see if I can grab a picture." Silver's phone was out. She scrolled through the pictures that she had taken. "I got the plate number. And I got a picture of the driver." She sent the photos off to Bill. "Let's see what he can do." She bit at her lip before she sent them off to Emma. "I'll send them off to Emma as well. She's been quiet so far."

"She has been. Richard mentioned that Abe's team has been out of town, not that they want to but they had to be. Emma was with them."

"That's what I wondered. This is hard too, Naomi."

"It is. This is where we need to trust God. It's hard at times, we both know that. This is one of those times too when our prayers are inaudible. God does hear us."

"He does." Silver still sat in the car, staring through the windshield. They were in the hospital parking lot. She sighed and reached for the door handle. Walking towards the building, she looked up to see Richard, Timothy, Stephen, and Bill heading her way. "What do they want?"

"Protecting you more than likely." Naomi linked an arm with hers. "Let them. We know how they work, and we can work with them. That's how they take care of us."

"I know. I just don't have to like it." Silver's eyes slid closed before she sighed. "I'm sorry. That's not really what I wanted to say."

"We understand that as well, Silver." Richard turned to walk with her, the other three men closing around her. "We've had word again about the danger that you are in. We're trying to determine who it is."

"Is it really drugs, Richard? That seems to be what they want us to think. What if it's something else? Or if it's drug, why a grow-op? Why not some designer drug or something like that? I think Sorley had talked to Bill about what he is investigating."

"He has, Silver, and there are some drug investigations in that, financial as you are aware. I can't go into more than that."

"I know, Bill. I'm just grasping at straws, trying to understand it all. And I'm too tired to absorb anything that you say to me."

"It's understandable, Silver. You haven't recovered from your poisoning. You're stressed because of Sorley. And there is the someone out there after you and Sorley who is still hidden and working to harm you."

"That about sums it up, Bill. I need to sleep and can't. Not while Sorley's here in the hospital. We'll see what happens when he goes home."

The men watched as Silver disappeared into Sorley's room. They shared a look, Bill walking away, heading towards Andrew.

"Bill? How is she?" Andrew's glance had followed Silver's path.

"Hurting, Andrew. She's barely staying on her feet."

"About what we expected. They're both in danger. I just wish we could solve this and now."

"So do I. We just don't have the information that we need. I've tried to find out what Dugan had and haven't been able to."

Silver stood beside Sorley, sorrowing that he was hurt. She just didn't know why and that frightened her. She didn't know where to turn any more, even though their families and friends were providing support.

This is where You step in, isn't it, God? You take our burdens and our stresses and bring us through them. We need to rely on Your strength. I'm scared, dear Lord. I want to be strong but feel so weak. I know that when we are weak, You make us strong. Please, Lord, heal my Sorley. Heal me. Help us to find the ones responsible and bring them to justice.

Chapter 30

Three days later, Sorley stood in the office in their home, hearing Silver moving around quietly in another room. She had stared at him when he headed for the office, knowing that there was work he needed to look at. She had sighed and walked away.

Sorley reached for the paperwork in his safe, thanking Silver for heading to the office for it. His secretary had dropped by and left more work for him before they had reached home. Sorley sat in his chair, booting up his computer and then reading his emails. He grinned suddenly, hearing from Emma. She had simply stated that she was working on their adventure. Did they really have to have one? He sent off a quick email back before he printed off the information that she had sent. Silver had appeared, working with him to collate the paperwork before she turned to him.

"Sorley, you can't put in a full day. Not yet. You just can't sit that long."

"I know, sweetheart. I won't. I just need to get a sense of what's out there. There were a couple of cases that were almost finished. I was just waiting for a couple of investigations to complete. If they are complete, I can finish them off and send them on to the investigators."

Silver nodded, having known that was the case.

"What can I do for you?"

"What can you do? You have good security clearance, don't you?" At her nod, he pointed to the computer monitor. "Okay, we work together on this. Then, you can watch me." He grinned as she shook a finger at him. "No? Okay, then I'll go through the emails, check my programs, send on what I need to. It should only take an hour or two. Then I will rest."

"I'll be back in ninety minutes, Sorley, and you will get up from there." She glared as he laughed and commented about being hen-pecked. "You are not. Behave yourself."

Sorley watched her walk away and then turned back to his work. He felt a hand on his shoulder later and looked up.

"Has time passed already?" He leaned back, groaning at the pain. "I have finished what I need to. The other investigations can wait until tomorrow." He was on his feet, drawing Silver towards him for a kiss.

Silver hugged him and then turned him away from the computer, tidying away his paperwork and locking it away for him. She wrapped an arm around him, holding on tight as his steps faltered. She refused to let him head for the living room, just for the bedroom. She settled him, handed him his pain medications, and then watched as he drifted off to sleep.

Silver turned from the bedroom, sobs catching her unawares. She was worn out but not ready to sleep herself. She instead headed for her laptop, working away in the living room, doing what she could for work, and then sending it on to Richard.

An email caught her attention and she read it. She replied before forwarding it to Bill and then

Richard. Emma had found information, she said, and would be sending it with one of their fellows on the next day. Each of them would receive copies. And just how was Silver doing? Did she need to talk with someone?

Silver set aside her laptop, stretching out on the couch. She slept, not hearing the knocking at the door. She wondered afterwards if she had would it have made any difference?

Sorley rose in the late afternoon, showered, shaved, and dressed in clean clothes. He hated the way the hospital smell lingered. He had not taken the time when he came home to do that. Sorley headed through the house, searching for Silver, just standing and watching her. He reached to kiss her and then headed for the kitchen. He glanced at the clock. It was mealtime. He grinned as he saw the crockpot plugged in. One of the mothers had been through and left a meal. Lifting the lid, Sorley drew in a deep breath, inhaling the aroma of the beef noodle soup. He felt a hand on his back and wrapped Silver into his arms.

"Feeling better, sweetheart?"

"Not really, Sorley. How are you?"

"I feel better now that I had a shower. I hurt and will but I am alive and with the love of my life." He kissed her and then stood and stared at her.

"That's good. Your mom brought that earlier. She says that they're doing meals for us over the next few days, between our families."

"They will take care of us. Let's eat. Then, we need to spend some time in prayer."

"We do." Silver moved away from him, finding the bowl and soup ladle, filling the bowls and handing them to him. "There's fresh bread as well, already sliced, your Moms said."

"That's good."

They ate and then bowed in prayer. When they finished, Sorley reached for her hand.

"Have you talked to anyone about what happened?"

"Not since this morning when you were working. Bill called. He's no further ahead, he said. There is a bit of information that they don't have and they need that. Emma's sending someone with information tomorrow. She didn't say how. I would suspect Murphy and Adriel."

"Why them?"

"Because Adriel is the one who was poisoned. Emma feels that we need to talk to them, to find out how they dealt with it and how their experience can help us."

"That would help. I'm lost right now on how to get through this."

"Me too." Silver rose to tidy the kitchen, her hand on his shoulder keeping Sorley in his seat.

"How be we head out to sit on the front porch? The sun usually doesn't shine on there quite as hot as the back porch."

"I can handle that." Silver reached for their mugs of coffee, heading for the door, waiting for Sorley to open it and then headed for the love seat there.

Sorley wrapped her in his arms, content and happy to be with her, even though the pain was starting up again. He watched the traffic on the street, not as much as there could be, including the odd patrol car that crawled past their home.

"Bill has sent them." Silver commented on the cars. "He said that he would for a couple of days."

"That's good." Sorley grew pensive, thinking through what had transpired and wanting it over. Only he knew that it would not be, not for a while.

Chapter 31

Richard frowned at Silver the next morning. She had appeared in his office, an envelope in her hand. She was furious, he could tell, and he had waved her to a seat.

"Silver? First, how is Sorley?"

"He's hurting but insisting on working. Sean and Seamus showed up. That's why I'm here. I found this." She shook the envelope that she held. "This! It was in the letterbox this morning. I have no idea when it was put there. Sometime over the last twenty-four hours is my guess. Do you know what it says?"

"No, I don't. Let me see it please." Richard reached for it, his eyes on Silver. He didn't think that he had ever seen her so distraught or so angry.

"They're threatening us, Richard. It's brutal. And we've seen brutal things in our day with our work."

"We have, but this is personal." Richard read it and winced. "No, they are not nice. It is brutal. Have you called Bill?"

"I have. He was tied up somewhere on some case as was Lily. He's going to stop by later. We've handled the letter. Sid was by and looked at it but couldn't find any evidence on it. I want this person."

"And we will find them. Now, what can I do for you?" He looked as the other three gathered in the office. "What can we do for you?"

"Find this person. And just how do we do that?"

"If it was someone that we were protecting, at this point they would be lining the walls with paper and working that way. We can do that." Timothy grinned at her scowl.

"We can. Can we meet tonight or tomorrow? No, it's Saturday, isn't it? You'll have plans."

"Our plans include you, Silver, and Sorley. We need to help you. This is one way that we can. We've been working on it on our own. It's time to collate what we've learned." Stephen leaned against the wall, his eyes steady on his friend. He was assessing her, seeing her become brittle from worry and fatigue.

"Emma said someone was heading our way today with information. We'll go over that." Silver was on her feet, moving away, a brief thanks floating behind her.

"She's stressed to the breaking point." Naomi finally spoke, her voice loud in the silence.

"She is. And we can't do much about that. She has to deal with that herself." Richard sat back, his eyes on his desk. "It's not just that she's in trouble. She's worried about Sorley. Being a newlywed is stressful enough. Having to deal with this? It's adding pressure that no one can ease until we find the ones behind it."

"We've been talking, Richard." Stephen spoke. "We think it's someone here in town."

"It always is. You have thoughts?"

Stephen nodded.

———

"We do. We've been looking into them. I reached out to Emma this morning, providing a list of names for her. She just emailed back a thanks and that she would look into them." Stephen walked away. He had information that he needed to work on and standing there just wasn't doing that.

Richard walked towards his home late that afternoon. He had been caught up with phone calls and requests that he had had to sort through. Most he had refused as they were requests to provide actual security service. Those he had directed to other teams who he was confident could handle the requests.

He looked up as he heard his name called.

"Abe? You're here?"

"I am, Richard. We need to talk." Abe waited as Richard unlocked his house. "Head off to clean up. I'll start our coffee."

Richard nodded, heading to change from the dress clothes he had pulled on that morning. He hesitated for a moment, praying for the unknown that had just happened. He walked back towards Abe, the cooler floor feeling comfortable to his bare feet. He reached for the meal in the crockpot, simply dishing up two plates.

After they had eaten, Abe studied his friend and then simply prayed for him, Richard's prayer echoing afterwards. Abe waited, not sure how to approach what he had to say.

"Abe? You're not here just for your health. I know you too well for that." Richard grinned for a moment before he sobered.

Abe smiled as he shook his head.

"No, I'm not. Murphy and Adriel met with Sorley and Silver today at our request. Emma sent information and I have the same packet for you. Bill has received one as well. She is deeply concerned at what she is finding."

"I thought that she would be, given that she sent you. What can you tell me?"

"Tell you? That Silver and Sorley walked into something that goes well beyond our borders. There is a drug smuggling ring operating out of the quarry in your area. They have hidden it well. The shack where they were kept? That was a meeting point for the mules."

"It was? We know there was no grow-op there despite the rumours about it. What kind of drugs are we talking about?"

"New stuff. Similar to what Bill and Cora faced. I spoke with Bill's brother, Wesley. He's no longer on that task force, had just left it in fact. He wasn't able to say much other than that they were aware of the rumours."

"And until we confirm them, it will just be rumours. It is a lucrative process, smuggling drugs. But I still think that something else is involved."

"And more than like there is. We just haven't found it out yet. We will though. I promise you that.

———

Listen, I need to run. We have a team in and plan an early morning. Go through what I left. Talk to Bill and Silver and Sorley. Call Emma. She's expecting you to do that."

"I will. Thank you, Abe. I know it went hard with you when your guys went through this. You did tell me at the time that when each one went through what they did that something seemed left over until it reached you."

"And there was. Emma's aunt's third husband. Another person to speak to would be Barnabas Carey. He went through the same thing. Every time one of his guys faced something, someone was also after him. Only it was to get to his father."

"I remember talking to him at the time. He said that. I'll speak with him."

Richard stood at his front door, locking it before he reached for his phone. He simply sent off a text to Silver, asking her to be very careful. He would talk with her and Sorley in the morning.

Silver read his text and then showed it to Sorley. He looked at her with a question on his face. Their meeting with Murphy and Adriel had greatly disturbed him.

Chapter 32

Silver drew in a deep breath the next morning. Sorley was still sleeping, and she had left him doing that. She moved through the house, knowing that she needed to work and not wanting to. She was worn out, she decided. Silver knew that she had never felt quite that bad before, even with the difficulties that they have faced as a team.

A tap at the door startled her enough that her hand flew to her mouth. She crept on almost silent feet to the front door and peeked out. A breath of relief wafted from her. Sean stood there.

Opening the door, Silver stared at him for a moment. Sean stared back, taking in the stress showing in his sister-in-law. He reached to hug her before moving her back from the door so that he could close it and then lock it.

"Silver? Did you get some sleep?" Sean watched her closely.

"I did, thank you. Sorley slept all night, which is a blessing."

"God was good then. Now, what can I do for you?"

Silver shrugged and turned, heading for the kitchen. She glanced at the clock before drawing in a deep breath.

"Sean? Aren't you working today?" She turned to watch him as he stood near the table.

"I work from home, Silver, doing IT work. I have my laptop with me. I've worked from here before. You need to be at work."

"I should go in. I've been doing some stuff that I need to give to Richard and go over it with him and the others."

"Head off then. I'll stay here for Sorley."

Richard looked around as he heard Silver's voice. He rose, walking to his office doorway, seeing Silver standing there, folders in her hand, deep in conversation with Timothy and Stephen. He waited, knowing that she would come towards him.

"Silver? Should you be here?" Richard raised his head from his work. He had returned to his desk, deep into what he needed to do as he waited for her.

"Richard, I need to be. Sean came by and offered to stay with Sorley. He'll call me if he needs to. I wanted to give you these." She passed over the folders that she was holding. "I've given copies to everyone else. Once you've read through them, we need to talk."

"What is this?"

"What I envision that I could do on the team. I don't know if that's what you were wanted but I thought it would help."

"It will, Silver. Now, about you? What can we do to help you?" Richard prayed for his friend.

"I don't know, Richard. Sorley and I talked about what has been happening. Well, as much as we could. He's hurting, Richard. He doesn't know who or why."

"None of us do. I had a meeting with Abe and he had some ideas."

"I'm sure that he did. He wants to tuck us away somewhere, doesn't he?" Her voice was disgruntled.

Richard grinned, waving at the other three to come on into the office.

"He didn't say that. He knows that won't work. Now, we want to work with you on that. We've been working on our own. It's time to meet and correlate everything."

Silver nodded, seeking each one of her friend's faces. She was grateful for them. Now, they wanted to meet and she was agreeable to that.

"Can we meet at our place?" Silver was hesitant to ask that.

"We can. How be we work through what we need to and then head that way?" Richard watched as the other four rose and walked away. He reached for his phone, needing to make some calls but still troubled about how the meeting had ended.

Silver ran for her house that afternoon, dodging the rain drops as she did so. She flew through the front door, shutting it behind her and locking it. She searched for Sorley, not finding him at first. She turned as she heard his voice and Sean's responding. She frowned as she heard another voice. Stopping in the office doorway, Silver stopped just short of the doorway. She didn't recognize the man who sat there although he looked familiar.

Sorley looked up as he heard Silver and then excused himself to find her. He simply wrapped her into his arms, knowing that they were both grateful to be together.

"Silver? You're okay? Sean said that you had headed into work."

Silver looked up at him.

"I did. The team is heading this way this afternoon, wanting to help work on our adventure, as they say." She looked around him. "Who's here?"

"Bill's brother, Wesley. He stopped by at Bill's request. He used to work on a drug task force."

"He did? Okay. So what has he said?"

Sorley turned her back to the office.

"Come and meet him."

"I have already, a while ago. Right now, Sorley, I'm just not up to it." Silver walked away, leaving him staring after her.

Wesley looked up as Sorley returned before glancing at the door. Silver didn't want to talk with him, he knew. He would just leave what he could for her and then walk away.

"Wesley? That last thought that you had?" Sean was studying his notes.

"About the smuggling? That. I can't say what all was involved but we did track the head person back to here. They were still working on finding all the information that they needed in order to make an arrest."

"And that you need. Okay." Sean's eyes met Sorley's. He nodded. They would go over it later.

Wesley rose, walking away, heading to find Bill. He had information that he could only pass on to law enforcement and right now, that was Bill.

Chapter 33

Silver reached for the roll of paper, working with Timothy to tape it to the walls. This was not the optimal way to do this but they had done it before for clients. She stepped back, a finger tapping at her mouth.

"How do you want to do this, Silver?" Stephen stood nearby, looking through the folders that he held.

"With the names, I think. Then, we'll fill in the basics." Silver leaned back against Sorley, knowing that he was behind her. "Sorley? Should you still be up?"

Sorley was in some pain but not enough to walk away from this. It looked too interesting.

"I'm fine, sweetheart."

"What are we doing? We don't have whiteboards as the police do. So, we use this. We've done it before with clients." She twisted to look up at him. "We'll need your input as well."

He grinned down at her, relishing the moment.

"Ok, I can do that. Now, how be we eat? Naomi and Richard have made a food run from Ev's."

"Food? Did you say food?" Silver gave him a quick hug and then headed for the kitchen, leaving him staring after her.

Timothy and Stephen began to laugh, drawing his attention to them.

"Did she just do that?"

"She did. A word of warning for you. Don't get inbetween Silver and food." Timothy continued to laugh as he moved past Sorley, finding Tate waiting for him.

Stephen was grinning and nodding as well.

"He's right. She can have a one-track mind sometimes when it comes to food." Stephen hesitated before he stopped beside Sorley. "How are you really doing, Sorley?"

Sorley shrugged, not quite sure how to respond.

"Okay, I guess. The pain is less. It's the mental and emotional sides that I'm trying to deal with. That's hard. That and trying to keep Silver safe, even though she has more training in that than I do."

"We need to find someone for you to talk to. That will help. As to keeping her safe? You do what you can, even though it is hard. You can't smother her. You have to let her make her choices. All you can do is be there for her and pray for her."

"That's true. She won't let me smother her. We've had discussions on that." Sorley hesitated. "She said that you're not going out on assignments any more?"

"That's correct. Richard has been thinking this way for a while."

"I can see why." Sorley hesitated to speak, not sure on how to phrase what he wanted to say.

"You want to ask something?" Stephen watched him closely, seeing the strain that he was under.

"I do. I know you would have already thought of it. Is there someone else after Richard? Some of the events don't seem to tie directly to myself or Silver."

Stephen was nodding. Sorley asked the question that they had all been asking.

"We think that there is. We just don't have enough information to determine if that is the case. It doesn't make it any easier for you."

"No, it doesn't." He reached to draw Silver close to him. She had come to look for him, not wanting to interrupt the two men. "Silver?"

"We know that there is someone. We just don't know who. You need to get sitting down, Sorley."

He sighed, knowing that she was correct.

Three hours later, Silver looked up, seeing that Sorley had simply laid down on the couch and was asleep. She rose to cover him with a blanket before walking from the office. She needed a break to think through what they had discovered.

Naomi watched her and then followed her, knowing that she didn't need to speak; she just needed to be there.

Silver stared out at the night. It was getting late and she needed to sleep. But she couldn't. Not while they were working on what they were.

"Naomi? Have we made any progress?"

"We have, Silver. We've been able to rule out our cases for the most part. There are one or two that we need to look deeper at. Richard has gone to Emma for that." Naomi stood shoulder to shoulder with her friend.

"That's what I thought. Now, how do we do this? Rule out others?" Silver tugged at her pony tail, a habit she had when she was deep in thought.

"That we do. We've passed on everything to Bill and Lily. We'll let them work away on that while we still do. Look, tomorrow is Saturday. What are your plans?" Naomi turned to her friend, wanting to take all the problems from her.

"I don't know. Sorley is not up to much, not right now. Our parents will be around on Sunday. I think tomorrow we just need to stay quiet." Silver bit at her lip, not sure what they were planning.

"I think that you do. If you need me, call me. I need to head out, Silver." Naomi hugged her friend and then walked away.

Silver turned as the men on her team surrounded her, praying for her. Timothy and Stephen walked away. Richard hesitated, not sure what to say to her.

"It's okay, Richard. We need to talk at some point, I think. For now, head on home. You have copies of what we were doing, I know." Silver hugged her friend and then locked the door behind him. She retraced her steps to the office, standing for a moment to study Sorley, wrapping her arms around herself.

She dropped to her knees beside him, wrapping an arm around him. Her head rested against him. She prayed for healing for him, knowing that this was not over. And she had no way of knowing how soon it would be.

Sorley stirred, hearing Silver's soft prayer. He reached for her, just holding her for a moment before he sat up, drawing her down beside him.

"Okay, sweetheart?"

"No, I don't think that I am." Silver studied him, seeing the pain on his face. "You need your medications, Sorley."

"I know. For now, let's just sit here. We need to pray for ourselves and for those involved. I fear that it's going to get a lot worse."

Chapter 34

A week later, Sorley headed into his office, greeting his secretary before he dropped his briefcase on his desk. He frowned at the piles of paper, knowing that he had work to do. He just didn't feel like doing it.

Three hours later, his head raised and his hand paused on the paper that he was reading. He was on his feet, recognizing Bill's voice.

"Bill? Come on back." Sorley waited for Bill to seat himself before he closed the door. "You're here?"

"I am, Sorley. I just wanted to touch base with you. How are you feeling?" Bill eyed him, seeing the slight wince from pain that the other man gave.

"I'm getting there. It does take time. I just want this over."

"We know that you do. We're working through it all, taking in what Emma has forwarded and what Silver and her team had unearthed." Bill studied his notes. "We're starting to arrest the lower level of the group. That will drive the head ones underground."

"And that is when it becomes more dangerous. Now, who do you want me to investigate for you?" Sorley grinned at Bill.

Bill began to laugh, a finger shaking at Sorley. He handed over a folder, a thoughtful look on his face.

"I can do that." Sorley squinted at the clock. "I can get a start on it today." He paused before he looked at Bill, finding himself watched intently. "I had a visit for your brother, Wesley."

"Did you? He was on the drug task force." Bill had already spoken with his brother, learning about their conversation.

"That's what he said. He had some good information for us. I just wish we didn't face all this."

"No one likes that. God has allowed it, Sorley." Bill bit at his lip. "I don't know if you know my story." Sorley shook his head, waiting for Bill to continue. "My first wife was killed by someone testing out a new designer drug. We didn't find that out for years. Elizabeth and I had only been married for six months. The one who gave it to her? Cora's first husband. He was killed on their wedding day, just as they left the church. Elizabeth had been stalked. Cora had been too. So, I have a vested interest in taking down any drug offenders."

Sorley's face grew sad as he listened.

"I pray that doesn't happen to myself or Silver. It's not how life is to be. But life happens. I firmly believe that God is in control."

"He is. We forget that. We need to step back sometimes and wait, knowing that He has only our good in place for us."

Bill rose at last, walking away, not content that he had reached through to Sorley. Sorley was a difficult read at times, he thought.

Sorley reached for his jacket at last, packing away what he needed to take home with him. He shut off lights on his way out and locked the door behind him. He frowned as he saw Stephen waiting for him.

"Stephen?"

Stephen grinned, pointing towards Sorley's car.

"I'm here to make sure that you get home safe. And yes, it's necessary." Stephen's eyes were in constant movement, guarding his friend's husband.

"I see. It's to that point, is it?"

"Not quite, but Richard felt it was necessary." Stephen shut his car door, waiting for Sorley to drive away. "Sorley?"

Sorley shook his head, not sure what to say.

"Thank you, Stephen. I know this is on your own time." His hand went up at Stephen's protest. "I appreciate it. Silver is not saying much but I gather this is what you all do."

"It is. Silver has been there for us. She was there with Timothy and Tate not that long ago."

"She was, wasn't she? Now, where is your car?"

"At your place. Timothy dropped me off at your office. One of us will drive in with you in the morning and back home at night. Just for now." Stephen sighed to himself, knowing it was up to him to explain why. "We've received new threats against you and Silver, Sorley. We have confirmed them. Bill is aware of them. He is having patrol officers come by your office and your home on a more regular basis. However, we can help by getting you and Silver to where you need to be. That's what we do, Sorley. It's our job. But more importantly, you are friends. Silver is a valued member of our team as well. We can't do less for you than we do for clients."

"No, I guess you can't." Sorley pulled to a stop in his driveway, parking beside Silver's car. "I just wish that you didn't have to."

"It's not a problem at all. Let's get you inside and then I'll walk your property again."

Sorley stared at him before he nodded.

"You need to do that, don't you? What else?"

"Richard is planning on dropping by this evening. Silver knows what to watch for and what to do. We just need to enlighten you on that." Stephen grinned again before he shut the door behind him, motioning Sorley to the house.

Sorley slowly shut the door behind him, hearing Silver singing to herself. She sounded happy and content. He smiled. This is what he had been missing for so many years. Someone to share his home and his life. He headed towards the kitchen, standing in the doorway, his eyes on his bride. He loved her deeply, more each day, and didn't know that he would have enough time in his life to tell and show her that.

Silver's hands paused as she prepared their salad, sensing someone behind her. She turned, a huge smile lighting up her face. The knife that she held dropped to the counter as she sprung towards him, to be caught close to his heart.

Silver spun, her feet almost tripping her up. She had slipped away for a few hours, heading for the downtown area. She wanted to find something for Sorley and had done that. Now, she was regretting coming here.

Running for her vehicle, Silver slid to a halt, seeing the man leaning against her car. She didn't know him. There would be no way that she would go to her car at this point. Her phone was out and she shot a number of photos, sending them on to her team and also Bill and Lily. Silver moved away, heading for Ev's diner, knowing that she would find refuge there. If she was fortunate, Avery, Andrew's cousin, would be working.

Hearing her name called, as she approached the diner, Silver spun, a hand to her throat. She relaxed as she saw Phoebe, Cora, and Madigan approaching her.

"Silver? You're here.? Cora grinned at her.

"I am. And so are you." Silver held the door for the others and then followed them to a booth.

"We are. We've been hoping to find you. Sorley just said that you were downtown and he didn't know why."

Silver laughed but the laugh didn't quite meet her eyes. The three other ladies exchanged glances.

"I was. I wanted to find something for Sorley. I did that. Only there was someone near my car. I didn't want to go there."

Cora reached to hug Silver.

"Do you have a photo?"

"I do." Silver showed the photo to the ladies.

"I know him." Madigan frowned for a moment. "Why is Dave here?"

"Dave?" Silver was puzzled

"Dave. He's from Riverville and is a friend of Abe's." Cora excused herself to head to where Dave was waiting.

"Dave?" Cora stopped in front of him. "Why are you here? And where's Rylee?"

"Rylee is in the diner. Abe sent me." He walked back towards the diner. "I didn't expect to find you here." He walked into the diner after her. Rylee waved from a table that she had chosen.

"Just let me grab the other three with me and we'll join you."

Silver studied the man who had appeared. She relaxed somewhat, knowing that Abe had likely sent him. Introduced to Dave and Rylee, she was still on edge.

Dave watched her, his eyes thoughtful.

"You're not from here?" Silver spoke at last.

"No, we're not. Abe sent me." Dave handed over a thumb drive. "He sent this. Emma didn't want to trust it to emails or couriers."

"And you've done this before?" Silver wasn't backing down from him.

"We have. Abe will use his circle of friends as he needs to. I'm not in law enforcement. I'm a paramedic. Rylee here runs a bakeshop."

Silver nodded, tucking away the thumb drive. She would look at it, discuss it with Sorley, and then pass it on to her team. There must be something there for Emma to take the steps that she had.

Sorley looked around from his work as he heard Silver moving towards him. He glanced at the clock. It was late afternoon by now. He had not expected her to be away that long. On his feet, he met her in the hallway, wrapping her in his arms.

"Okay, sweetheart?"

"I am, now that I'm with you." Silver held up the gift bag. "This is for you."

"It is? What did you get me?" Sorley peeked into the bag. "What's this?"

"It's the devotional book that you wanted. I had to find it for you." That earned her a long kiss. "Now, I do have something else to talk to you about."

"We will. For now, we need to just set everyone aside for an hour or two." Sorley turned her away from the office. "We'll eat and then spend some time together. We need that."

"We do, my love." Silver set aside the thumb drive, a thoughtful look on her face. "Emma sent it with a friend of theirs."

"She did? Then it is important. But not as important as you. We'll get to it, sweetheart."

Silver nodded, knowing that he was correct.

"We'll do that. I set a casserole in the oven before I went out. It should be ready." She opened the oven door, waving at the heat that escaped, causing Sorley to begin laughing.

Two hours later, refreshed from their meal and the Bible study and prayer time that they had taken the time for, they headed for the office.

"Okay, Silver. Where's your thumb drive?" Sorley reached for it, turning it over and over in his hands.

"I don't know what's on it. I'm not sure that I want to. Apparently, Bill has the information as well. We'll need to look at it and then pass the information on to my team."

"How is it going with the plans to change the focus of your team?" Sorley worked away, loading the information from the thumb drive to his computer.

"It's going good. It is a niche that is needed. There are so many teams out there that are only partly trained. Richard made sure that we had training before we went out on our first assignment. I appreciate that about him."

"He is thorough. He thinks through everything."

"He does." Silver perched on the edge of the chair that she had dragged up beside Sorley's. "What do we have?" Her eyes widened as Sorley began to scroll through the information.

"This is interesting, sweetheart. How does she find this?"

Silver shrugged, not sure how to respond.

"She just does. She has an incredible memory and can make connections between people, addresses, and cases without any effort. She also can't explain how she does it."

"I need to meet this lady." Sorley's attention shifted from the computer to Silver, seeing the intentness with how she was reading the material.

Chapter 36

Silver's head came up from her work the next morning, hearing Richard's voice as he entered the office. She had been there for a while, wanting to use the resources that were available there. A copy of the thumb drive sat on Richard's desk, ready for him.

Richard picked up the thumb drive before he turned to the door. Silver had been in early, he knew, having seen her arrive. He would talk to her soon, he decided. Right at the moment, he had phone calls and emails to answer.

Two hours later, Silver tapped at his door, a folder in her hand.

"Richard? Who is this?" She handed over the folder. "It says that they employed here. But they're not."

Richard's hand stilled for a moment before he took it, his eyes on Silver.

"Silver?"

"I have a bad feeling about this. He's not one of ours. I don't recognize his name." Silver slipped into a chair, her hands clasping and unclasping.

Richard read through the material before he read through it again, this time with his pen making notes. Reaching for the computer mouse, he woke up his computer and input the name. Sitting back, he frowned at the monitor before frowning at Silver.

"I don't know who this is. This is a plant, Silver. I want to know why."

"Me, too. I didn't recognize the name. I also couldn't find anything on him."

"No, I couldn't either. And we should do. That means it's a fake name."

Silver paled, knowing that Richard was correct.

"Is he one of the head ones who are after us?"

Richard shrugged, not sure how to answer that.

"I don't know, Silver. I'll pass it on to Bill. He'll make it part of the investigation."

"I know he will." Silver slumped back into her chair. "Am I bringing danger to us here? Do I need to quit?"

"No, you are not quitting. And I don't think that you are bringing danger to us. This may not be related to you at all. It's just bizarre. That's all."

Richard was on his feet, his hand on Silver's arm drawing her to her feet.

"Head on home, Silver. It's getting late in the day." Richard walked her out and then went over to her car, even though he knew that she would have done that. He watched her drive away, troubled by what she had discovered. He had to set it aside for then, knowing that he had a meeting at the church to get to.

Silver curled up in a chair in Sorley's office. He had not arrived home yet and had called to say that he would pick up a meal for them. She was grateful for that. She was exhausted, she decided, and needed to do something fun. Only doing that might bring more danger to them. She slept, her lack of sleep catching up with her. Silver was on edge all the time and trying to sleep had been difficult.

Sorley set down the bags of food, turning to thank Timothy for his help. He locked the doors and then went searching for his bride. He stood, a sad smile on his face. He reached to tuck a blanket around her and then turned, heading back for the kitchen. Sorley stared down at the food before he set it away in the fridge. He wasn't hungry, he decided, and would wait for Silver. Changing into casual clothes, he headed for the back deck, just to stand and stare around. Something felt off but he had no idea what it was.

Dusk fell and still Sorley stood on the deck, lost in thought and then in prayer. He grew quiet at last, his heart just being still in the presence of his God. He needed that, he knew, needed it to find the strength for the next week or so. He didn't think it would be much longer but he had no idea if it would take more than that. Bill had been around that morning, questioning him once more on one of the cases. Sorley had given him what information that he could, knowing that he couldn't give a lot. He had simply told Bill who to speak with.

Silver roused at last, seeing the low lights that were on. She sighed. Sorley was home, and here she was asleep. She was on her feet, searching for him, stepping at last out onto the deck. Seeing a familiar dark form standing there, she moved towards him, to be wrapped into his arms.

"Sorley? How long?" Silver leaned against him, hearing the sounds of night in her ears.

"How long? I'm not sure, sweetheart. I don't even know what time it is. I found you sleeping and didn't have the heart to wake you up."

"That's okay. But you brought a meal for us."

"It's in the fridge. I didn't feel like eating." He turned them for the house, locking up after them. "I can reheat it if you want."

Silver yawned, shaking her head.

"I'm not really hungry, but you are."

It was Sorley's turn to shake his head.

"I'm not either. Not now. Head off for bed, sweetheart. I'll be along shortly."

Silver walked away, crawled into bed and was sound asleep before she realized it. Sorley stared down at her, disturbed that she was so tired. He looked up, staring at the photo of a waterfall hanging above the bed. *This has to end,* he thought. *Only, I have no idea how to end it. Lord, please? Can we end this now? I want to go on living a life with my bride, and this is standing in our way.*

Sorley sat up abruptly in the night, rubbing at his eyes. He was on his feet, the blankets thrown back, as he stalked through the house, searching for what had awakened him. Standing near the back door, he listened to the low gruff conversation between the two men. They were standing where they would not be picked up on the security cameras. He reached for his phone, holding it to the door and recording what was being said, hoping that he could do that. He just wasn't sure that he could.

He felt a hand on his back. Silver had awakened and come to find him. Her hand stayed where it was even as she strained to listen. She nodded. She knew the one voice. He was a man who lived on the streets, on the wrong side of the law. It was known that he was deep into the drug trade.

Chapter 37

Running for Richard's building, Bill shoved open the door and let it close behind him. The suddenness with which he appeared startled the five team members, who rose and came towards him.

"Bill?" Richard's voice was stern and a frown covered his face.

"Richard? Good. You're all here. Where can we meet? I have some things that I need to discuss with you. Silver, I have someone with Sorley and that will continue for the next two weeks."

Silver was startled and then nodded.

"I see. We're getting that close?"

"We are. Now, let's find our seats and work through this."

Richard nodded, pointing towards the conference room.

"In there, Bill. We were just about to break for lunch. Will you join us?"

Bill nodded, knowing that there would be plenty to eat. He sat back at last, wiping his mouth on his napkin, a nod to Richard. They bowed in prayer for a while, knowing that they needed it.

Bill straightened back up, reaching for his briefcase. He pulled out folders and then handed around papers.

"I can give you this much. It is public knowledge and I have talked with the judge and he has authorized its release to you."

Hands reached for the papers and there was silence in the room except for the slight sound of rustling papers. Silver looked up at last, staring at the window across from her. She sighed. This just made it so much worse, she decided.

"Richard? What are your thoughts?" Bill watched him closely, seeing the stress that this meeting was causing.

"I don't know, Bill. I know this individual. I wouldn't have expected this person to be involved in drugs. Not given the history of her family."

"I know. There is a history there but we can look past that for now. What are your thoughts, everyone?"

Timothy had read back through the information. Familiar with the woman, he had other thoughts.

"She is involved and has been for years. There were rumours when I was in high school that she was supplying drugs and alcohol to the teens." He looked around, seeing Richard nodding. "We've talked about that many times, Richard."

"We have, Timothy. We know the undercurrents in our town. She is one of those. If we can put her away, that would be good." Richard looked around at his team. "Not all of you are from here. Stephen and Naomi, you're from nearby towns. You may not have heard of her. She is one who is prominent in town, fighting against drugs. But she has likely been dealing them for years behind the scenes.”

“That makes sick sense, you know.” Naomi shook her head. “How many times have we seen this?”

“Too many.” Bill looked back up from his paperwork. “What are your thoughts further on this? Anyone that she’s been seen with that you can name?”

Richard and Silver shared a look and then looked at Timothy.

“There are names that we can give. A number of them in fact.” Silver reached for a paper, writing rapidly and then passing it to Timothy.

Timothy read the list, added to it, and then passed it over to Richard. Richard’s keen eyes studied his friends and then the lists. He nodded as he read it. He added a few more, studied it once more, and then handed it to Bill.

“Here you go, Bill. I think this might help. I pray that it does. We need to end this and soon.” He had seen the stress that was wearing at Silver.

“We are working on that, Richard. The next week is crucial to our investigations. You are well aware that this is when it becomes the most dangerous. Silver, we need to protect you. How do we do that?”

Silver shrugged, not sure what to say. She was well aware that the forces after her were closing in and that made her afraid. She was also deeply afraid for Sorley, knowing that he was at risk as well. Not that they knew why. They had not been able to determine that. She just didn’t think that drugs were the reason.

"What if drugs are not the reason, Bill? We've been looking at that. But sometimes that is just a red herring."

"We thought of that, Silver. We are looking at other reasons. We need to find that one piece of information that would solve this."

"And we don't have that." Silver blew out a breath, desperate to find that one piece. "So what do we have then?"

Answers began to fly before Timothy was on his feet, scribing everything on the whiteboards. He stepped back for a moment, studying it. His eyes focused on a name. Reaching with a red marker, he circled the black handwriting. He turned as he heard a gasp. Silver was staring at him in horror.

"Him? He's been friends with us." Her horrified glance turned to Richard, who was on his feet, consternation on his face.

"Him?" Richard paced out of the room and then back in, a folder in his hand. He handed it to Bill, who studied it and then nodded.

"You've had suspicions in the past, Richard."

"I did. He seemed too interested in one of the assignments that we were going on. He pushed for information, which we would never give. I never trusted him after that but I had no reason to say anything."

"He has done that, I think, on purpose. We'll take a deeper look at him." Bill studied each one of them. "I won't tell you what to do. You know best how to protect yourselves and one another. If you see either one of these people or their spouses, call me or Lily or Andrew. They are aware of what's happening."

Bill walked away, stopping to stare up at the sky. He watched the clouds passing by, thinking that was how this case felt, that clouds were covering something up. He paused, his thoughts muddled, until he had a moment of clarity. He spun to stare at the office building before he was running for his car and heading for the office. There was a search that he needed to run and run at that very moment.

Chapter 38

Sorley reached for Silver's hand as they walked in a park near their home. They had needed to get away but not too far. She sighed as she looked around her. They were being followed, only she didn't know by whom.

Silver looked up at Sorley, finding his concentration elsewhere. He was worried, she knew. They wanted this over but had no way of ensuring that would happen very quickly.

"Sorley, what are your thoughts?"

"About what we're going through?" At Silver's nod, he sighed. He felt that they were at the crux of the investigation but didn't know who to watch out for. "I wish it was over, sweetheart. I want to go on with our lives and it's difficult to do."

"I know." Silver's steps slowed as she eyed the man in front of her. "Sorley, I think that we're in trouble."

He looked down at her and then up. *She's right, Lord. We are in trouble. And I don't know how to get us out of it.*

His hands rising, Sorley walked slowly forward, Silver in front of him. Forced to walk away from the entrance to the park, he felt a sense of having already done this. Silver's feet slowed as she approached the men waiting for her. She knew them. Why are they here?"

"Murphy? What are you doing here? And in the park?" She dropped her hands to reach for Sorley's hand. "Sorley, these are some of Abe's men. I know that you haven't met them. I just don't understand."

"Emma was worried too much for Abe to ignore her. He sent us four to find you. I'm sorry that we scared you. Doug there volunteered to come with us. I don't know if you've met him before."

"No, I haven't but I've heard of him. Okay. So, what do you want? We're not leaving our home. And you had better have talked to Richard."

"He has, Silver." Richard's voice sounded behind her, the other three members of her team with him. "We need to get you two out of here and to safety."

"I knew you would want to do that, Richard. I'm not ready to do that. Not until you explain." Silver was digging in her heels, voicing her feelings. It was what they had expected from her.

"We'll explain, Silver. You know better than to stand out here arguing with us. Let's move." Murphy's voice snapped at her, not his usual demeanour. He could feel evil closing in and didn't want to see a friend and her partner killed.

"I'm sorry, Murphy. Where do you want us?" Silver reached for Sorley's hand and walked after them, Richard and her team following them.

Heading for a secondary entrance to the park that wasn't as well used or known, Murphy simply pointed at their vehicles. Seated in Murphy's vehicle, Silver studied the men with her. Joseph was behind the wheel, Ian and Luke with them. She shifted closer to Sorley. Sorley didn't know these men but knew that Silver and Richard's team did. He trusted them because of that.

"Murphy? What did Emma find?" Silver's voice broke into the silence.

"She found the ones who are after you both. She has passed that on to Bill and Lily. But she doesn't want you two out there in the open. You know how it works only too well."

"I do. This is where we would move in as a team and put the endangered party into protective custody. It's different when it's you that the endangered party."

"It is, Silver." Ian spoke up. "We've all been there, as you know. Doug as well."

"I know. I heard about Doug's story. That was brutal." Silver caught the look on Sorley's face and gave a brief rundown of what had happened to Doug.

"He went through that? And all of you as well? How did you do it?" Sorley eyed each of the men. Doug had gone with Richard.

"With God's help, Sorley." Luke shifted to watch behind them, seeing Richard's vehicle there. "We would not have survived if we hadn't had that faith."

"That's what I don't get. How do people with no faith get through this?"

Silver watched as Joseph slowed to turn into a farm. She sighed. *Here we go, Lord. Timothy didn't have to do this but he's torn from Tate because of me. And I don't like that. It shouldn't be happening but it is. You have allowed this. Help me to find peace in this and be the witness that I need to be to those around me, even to those who are Your children.*

Sorley watched with interest as three of the men exited the vehicle, leaving Joseph behind the wheel. He wasn't sure why that was but everyone seemed to accept that.

"This is what we do, Sorley. You're getting a crash course into my work." Silver wrapped an arm around his. "We, the endangered parties, stay in a vehicle with a driver behind the wheel. That's in case someone appears and we need to be taken somewhere quickly. Joseph will not turn off the ignition. That is in case he needs to get us away and do that quickly. The others search to ensure that there isn't something here that would track us, harm us, or kill us."

Sorley nodded slowly. He was getting a crash course in her line of work, not one that he had really wanted. But it did help him to understand her better.

"I need to work, Silver. I have investigations that are running that I need to follow."

"And you'll be able to." Joseph spoke up. "Richard will have a laptop that you can use to access your programs. It will be a secure one that can't be hacked or traced. Silver? What can we get for you?"

Silver shrugged, knowing that as much as she wanted to be part of her team, she couldn't. She had to step back and let them work.

———

"Just a Bible, I think, Joseph. I can spend the time studying all the verses on protection that I can find. That will take some time."

Joseph nodded, a sad smile crossing his face. He didn't wish this on anyone, having gone through something similar. He knew that Silver and Sorley wanted to get on with their lives but just couldn't, not with this hanging over them.

Silver watched the others moving around, waiting patiently for the word to come that they could go inside the house and at least be able to move around. But she knew that even moving around outside would not happen. They just couldn't take a chance of being found. And that had happened too many times.

Chapter 39

Wandering through the downstairs of the farm house, Sorley noted that it was furnished comfortably. He just wanted to be in his own home, alone with Silver. He understood the need for the others to be there. Richard and his team were meeting, Silver with them. Murphy and the others had already left, promising to return if they were needed. He had watched Silver, seeing how she struggled to hide her feelings. He had wrapped her into his arms, his eyes on the vehicle as it left.

Richard had watched the pair, knowing that this was the crisis. If they did something wrong or missed something, these two may well die. And he didn't want that. Timothy had stared at them as well, missing his Tate but knowing that she would want him here to take care of their friends.

Stephen walked towards Sorley, needing to ask him questions but not sure how the questions would be taken.

"Sorley? Can you sit with me for a moment? I need to ask some questions that I am not sure if you can or will be able to answer."

Sorley sat, his eyes on Stephen.

"Stephen? What do you need to know?"

"We know that you work as a finance investigator. How do you find the answers that you are looking for?"

"How do I do it? I'm not sure that I can exactly explain it. I am given a name and the information that I need. I start by searching financial records from various sources and then just expanding my search outside of the country and then overseas. It's complicated in how I find the information. How does that apply to this?"

"We're just grasping at straws, I guess. We know that you would have looked into those names and their families. We won't ask you to compromise anything in your investigations. We're just trying to determine if someone would know if you're investigating them or something like that."

"They shouldn't be able to know that I am. It's all done under the radar, as you would say." Sorley thought through the investigations that he had done. "If someone who knew them had asked for the investigation or knew about it, they could say something. I know that has happened in the past to friends of mine. That had compromised the investigation."

"And we don't want that to happen. We have been careful, as you know, so that we don't ask for any information that you can't give. We need to keep that confidentiality. And Bill has been careful not to ask or say anything that would do the same."

"It's how it goes. If you think someone has said something, then talk to Bill. Someone on the force may have come up with an idea that they're being investigated and then talked out of turn."

Stephen nodded before he rose. His mouth opened as he went to say something before he snapped it closed and walked away, leaving Sorley with a frown on his face.

Silver slipped to a seat beside him, finding herself wrapped close to him. She never tired of being held by him.

"Stephen asking hard questions?"

"He is. He asked how I did my investigations. I can't give a lot of details."

"We know that, my love. We know that. Stephen is content with just generalized information. We all are. It's just trying to understand if what you can find would help solve this." She leaned against him. "Richard talked to our families."

"He did? They are safe?" Sorley had been worried about that.

"They are. They don't like that they have to hide but it's what is necessary at this point."

"I wondered if they had been tucked away. Thank you, sweetheart." Sorley's voice died away. His fatigue had caught up with him, still not back to his full strength. "Do we stay here for the duration?"

"Hopefully, but we may need to move. So just be prepared to move suddenly. Naomi took my keys and packed us a couple of bags."

"Did she? We'll need to do something to thank them."

"And we will. But for now, we need to be the protected parties. And I'm not sure that I can."

"You have your weapon?" Sorley felt Silver nod. "And you will use it if you have to, won't you?"

"If I need to. I pray that I never had to do so. I haven't had to yet, even though we have been under fire at different times. It's so final to shoot someone."

"It is. Now, how do we put in our time?" Sorley was thinking of the work that he had pending and needed to proceed with.

"Richard has a laptop that you can use, if you can access your programs. If you need anything packed up from your offices, let him know. One of them will do that for you."

"I can do that. For now, we relax, correct? Who's on dinner duty?" He grinned as she elbowed him.

"I'm not sure but we can do that if you want. This house has been stocked with food and Timothy did a run for fresh food." Silver was on her feet, her hand reaching for Sorley's.

Sorley listened to the teasing among the team and felt an outsider for a moment. He shouldn't, he knew; they had worked together for so long. Silver watched him, a hand on his. They tried to draw him into the conversation but he rose instead. He walked away, leaving them staring after him. He sat on the side of the bed in the room they had been assigned, his head bending as he prayed. He needed that time with his God. He turned as he heard Silver's laughter and was thankful that she was in his life. It was not how he had expected to find his life mate but God had chosen that way for him.

Chapter 40

Spinning around, Sorley searched for the source of the noise that he was hearing. He couldn't see anything but that didn't mean something or someone wasn't there. He heard running footsteps and spun once more, seeing Silver running towards him, a weapon in her hand. He reached for her free hand, following as she ran for the door and out of it, finding her team waiting for her. They ran for the trees, disappearing in them. Sounds of car doors slamming reached to them as they ran deeper into the woods.

His hand raised, Richard stopped the group in a small clearing, pointing at Timothy who nodded and headed back the way that they had just come. He would watch for anyone heading their way. He knew that if the team moved on, Richard would leave signs for him to follow.

Sorley breathed heavily, a hand to his abdomen. The running had set off the pain in his incisional area, not so bad that he couldn't continue but bad enough that he knew that he needed to rest. His eyes narrowed as he watched the team, seeing them for the first time in work mode. Silver stood beside him, Naomi nearby. Stephen had disappeared down the trail away from them. He reappeared and nodded at Richard.

Richard pointed towards Stephen, indicating that they should follow him. They took off at a fast walk, Richard bringing up the rear of the group. He turned as he heard footsteps, finding Timothy catching up with them.

"Timothy?" Richard kept his voice low.

"They're still at the house. I don't think they'll follow us. They don't seem to know what they're doing. I wouldn't suggest that we hang around here for too long."

"No, we won't. Stephen's leading us to somewhere. Hopefully, we'll be able to reach Bill or Andrew and then get a ride."

"I hope so. But I wouldn't count on that. We're outside of town and that's outside of their jurisdiction. I don't know that I want to go to another force."

"If we have to, we'll reach out to Wesley. He's on the Oak City force but can step in as a friend. Or I'll call Don. He's around this week."

"We may need to go that route." Timothy watched Silver, seeing how she had dropped into work mode. "Silver in work mode will be a surprise for Sorley."

"It will be but it's what's needed." Richard moved ahead quickly, passing the others to walk near Stephen.

Silver watched him and then the area around her. This was not how the day was to have gone. It was nearing dusk. They had run without being able to bring any supplies. That was not how it was to have been.

"Silver?" Sorley's voice was low. "Where are we heading?"

Silver shrugged, not sure herself.

"I don't know. We're hoping to find shelter somewhere and some food and water. It depends on if we are followed. So far, I don't think that we are."

"I pray that we're not. How long do you think?" Sorley shook his head. "Forget I asked that. You wouldn't have any idea."

An hour later, Richard stopped their forward walk once more. He eyed the house in front of him. He knew the owners, knew where they hid a key. He could use it. He just wasn't sure that he wanted to. He spoke quietly to Stephen and the two men moved forward quickly.

Silver watched them before her attention was on the area around them, just as she knew that Naomi and Timothy were watching. Sorley had sat on a tree stump, a hand to his abdomen. The incision was burning and sore. He needed to rest but didn't know if he would get that chance.

Richard was back quickly, a backpack in his hand. He handed out bottles of water and then packs of crackers.

"This is all that I dared take. The owner is known to me. He wouldn't say no but I don't want to stay here." He looked around and then up at the sky. It was drawing close to night and he wanted to find shelter for them. "We'll rest for about thirty minutes and then move out again. There are some cabins around here that I am familiar with where we can find shelter. Timothy? Do you know the area?"

Timothy nodded, familiar with the area. He had had friends from here. He also knew of a cabin that was well hidden, belonging to a friend.

"There's a cabin about an hour from here, Richard. It's well hidden. Unless you know where it is, you won't find it. It belongs to a friend's family. We can use it."

Richard nodded, pointing towards the path.

"When we walk off, Timothy, you take the lead. Stephen, you're at the tail."

Walking off at last, Sorley's steps were slow. He was tired, yet determined to keep up with his friends. Silver reached for his hand, her touch giving him the strength that he needed to go forward.

Richard watched him closely from where he had taken a position behind them. He was worried that Sorley would give out on them. He watched Silver as well, seeing the fatigue on her face but knowing that she would push through to get them to safety. It's what they all did.

Timothy stopped, his eyes on the cabin. It was still as hidden as always. He just didn't know if they should use it. He didn't have a good feeling about it. He waited before he saw a man peering around the edge of the cabin. He turned to find Richard beside him.

"We can't use it, Richard. It's been compromised. I would like to know how."

"Whoever it is has researched all of us and found out who are friends are. Now where do we go?"

Richard looked around, knowing that they needed to find shelter for the night.

"There are some caves near here. They have entrances at the back as well as the front. We used to ride dirt bikes out here when I was a teen. We explored them." Stephen pointed off to his right. "I know some paths that we can use. We need to get Sorley somewhere that he can relax."

"That we do. Lead on, Stephen. Timothy, you're at the tail again." Richard walked away after Stephen, hearing the soft sounds of the others following him.

Stephen stopped after about thirty minutes, a hand stopping the rest. A quiet word with Richard and they moved away, searching out the caves and walking through them.

"This will work for the night, Stephen. Come morning, we'll be up and away as soon as we can. The entrances are well hidden."

"They are. Unless you know where they are, you won't find them." Richard turned back to face the others. "Go and bring them here. I'll wait."

Stephen was away and back again with the rest, leading them to the caves. Richard assessed each one as they passed him, seeing the strain and tiredness of their faces. He knew that they would work in teams over the night, two at a time, keeping an eye out for danger. He would be up and around himself for the whole night. It was how he did it.

Chapter 41

Dawn found the group on their feet, moving through the back of the cave and out into a meadow. Timothy led the way, familiar with the area. Stephen was on the tail, watching closely for anyone who might appear. He was tired, as they all were. He just prayed that they found safety soon. He had watched Sorley overnight, seeing the pain on his face.

Silver was worried about Sorley. His steps were slow that day. She knew that he had slept, but his sleep had been broken. She herself had not slept much. She never did when she was on duty. Her team had been on duty that night, even though she was one of the ones that needed protection.

Sorley stumbled as he walked, finding Silver's hand reaching for his. He was grateful for her grip, helping him to walk forward. The pain was increasing and that worried him.

Richard watched him closely before he looked around him. They were coming close to civilization. He just prayed that they were. He needed to get the couple somewhere that was safe. He didn't feel safe out in the open like this.

Timothy stopped at the edge of a group of trees, studying the area around him. They had made their way back to Elmton, on the other side from where they lived. He was grateful for that. Now, they could find transportation and get Silver and Sorley to safety. He just didn't know where that way.

Richard paused at his side, his eyes in contact motion.

"We're back in town, Timothy. Now, we need to get somewhere."

"I know. Who do we call?"

"Call Silas. He's usually around the church at this time. He can bring the large van that we'll all fit into. And then we head for Bill. Someone sold us out and I want to know who." Richard was angry that they had been found.

"I sent off a text to Silas when I stopped, asking that. I also sent one off to Bill. He's gotten back to me. He wants us at the station."

Silver slid onto a van seat beside Sorley, her eyes on him before they raised to Stephen. Stephen nodded, knowing that Silver wanted him to assess Sorley. That he could and would do when they were in a safe spot.

Bill stood in the police department parking lot, watching as the group made their slow way towards him. Silas had dropped them off and then driven away, heading for the church and the duties that he had gladly set aside to help his friends.

"Richard? What happened? And why is Silas bringing you here?" Bill had not known that the group had been on the run without transportation.

"It's a long story, Bill. Our safe house was found and we barely had time to escape it. We've been walking all this time back from it. We spent time in a cave overnight. Sorley needs to be assessed. Silver is terrified even though she is covering it well. We're tired, sore, and angry. And Silas gladly picked us up near the edge of town and brought us here. We have a leak somewhere." Richard's face and voice were grim.

Bill nodded. They had discovered that only in the last hour. He had been unable to reach out to Richard, his calls not being answered.

"We found that out, Richard. I've been trying to reach you without success." Bill pointed to a small conference room. "In there. I'll have Lily make a food run for you. We do have coffee and tea." Bill waited as the door closed before he turned to find Andrew, who was not in the slightest pleased at the turn of events.

"Where are they, Bill?" Andrew sat back in his chair, his eyes on the paperwork cluttering his desk.

"In the small conference room." Bill sat for a moment. "We've been moving up the chain of command in our investigation. We should be ready to make arrests within the next twenty-four hours of those at the top. We just need to keep Silver and Sorley safe until then. This complicates it."

"Their families are safe?"

"They are. Abe and Don are helping out with that. They are tucked away out of town."

"Good." Andrew rubbed at his cheek, trying to come up with a plan that would work. He just wasn't sure that they could come up with one. "What are your thoughts, Bill?"

"I need to pull in the suspect and interview him. Jason is willing to do the interview. Lily is heading out with the arrest and search warrants that are needed. I won't do the interview. I'm too close to Richard."

"No, you can't. They could claim bias if you did. Okay. Keep me in the loop as to what is going on." Andrew watched as Bill walked away, troubled about Silver. She had become a good friend of theirs as had all of Richard's team. He wanted this over for them as well without any more harm coming to them.

Sorley looked around, almost too tired to think. He needed to work, his investigations at a point where he had to. He didn't have any choice in that.

Richard had been watching him, seeing the fatigue on his face. He turned to Bill, making a simple request. Bill shot a look at Sorley and nodded. He left and returned with a laptop which he handed to Richard.

"It's a secure one, Richard. No one can track it. Listen, Ev is sending in a meal for you all. Then, we have cots that will be brought in. Catch what rest you can. I will have an officer at the door. He'll come and find me if you need anything."

"Thanks, Bill. This is appreciated. Hopefully, we'll get this over with soon, and Silver and Sorley can get on with their life. I just pray that the rest of us don't go through what they did.

"I'm sure that you will. We can keep them here for now, but we will need at some point to get them home."

"And if you don't find everyone before that, then they are still at risk." Richard folded his arms across his chest, deep in thought. "How sure are you that you have identified everyone?"

Silver had approached them, listening to their conversation. Richard had stated what she was afraid of. She wanted to go home but was afraid too. And she didn't do fear all that well, she had discovered.

"Bill, will you be able to arrest everyone?" Silver's voice had fear, something the two men didn't think that they had heard before.

"We think so, Silver. We need twenty-four hours. We won't keep you here that long, though. Get some rest and then we'll see about getting you home late today." Bill nodded towards Sorley. "Your guy is hurting but needs to work."

"He is hurting. He has some work that he needs to do that he can't put off. He'll want to do that before he rests. Stephen had taken a look at the incision. If we can get some pain medications for him, that would help."

Chapter 42

Silver walked through their home late that night. Sorley had finally nodded his head, the pain driving him to walk slowly away from her, to crawl into bed. They had both showered and dressed back in clean clothes. Sorley simply didn't bother changing into his night clothes. He was just too tired to do so. He had finished the investigation that he had needed to. It had been on the head person in their own adventure. Sorley has turned over his information to Bill, who had taken it with thanks, knowing that Sorley would have been thorough. He had Lily verifying everything that Sorley had found

Standing watching Sorley sleep, Silver wept. It had just all culminated in her feeling defeated and sad. She didn't think that she had ever felt that low in her life. She turned from the bedroom, seeking the chair in the office that she had claimed, wrapping herself in a blanket. Her thoughts turned to God and His protection. That they had felt in a new way that day. She knew that they should not have escaped and should not have found a hiding place where they had been safe. God had arranged that for them, she acknowledged. She was always amazed and humbled at how God would work. Richard would have agreed with her, she knew. So would Sorley.

Her thoughts then turned to the person whom they suspected. She frowned for a moment, tracing the woman's family and then her extended family. She wondered how far it extended. This woman had been in business in town for as long as Silver could remember. And that meant that she likely had a good source of material and people whom she could turn to. Silver's head went down on the back of the chairs, drifting off to sleep. Her body needed that.

Neither heard the footsteps around their house that night. Nor did they hear the rattling of the doorknobs. The woman they were running from had taken matters into her own hands. She tried to find a way inside but was thwarted. She cursed and turned away, a black evil look covering her face. The evil that she had lived with for so many years was destroying her and it showed in her features. Her family looked at her and then turned away. Her three children had learned early to avoid her. When her husband walked away from her, they went with him. They had no contact with her at all. For that reason, she blamed everyone else, not seeing that it was she herself that had ruined her life.

The next morning, Silver moved through the house, opening the drapes, turning on the coffee, and then turning to find Sorley behind her. She reached for him, content and safe in his arms. They stood for a number of moments, just holding one another before Sorley stood back.

"What's on for today, sweetheart?"

"I have no idea. Richard will be around at some point, I suspect, to guard us. Bill had a patrol officer outside last night." She frowned. "Except the car isn't there now and it should be." She reached for her phone. "Bill? No, we're okay. I have a question for you. Didn't you have a patrol officer parked outside last night? That's what I thought. I don't see the car now. They should still be here, shouldn't they?"

Bill was on his feet, heading for his car as he called for a patrol officer to head for Sorley's house. His door slammed behind him as he rushed towards the house. The patrol officer shrugged, not finding the car or the officer.

"Where is he, Bill? Rod would not have left. He's too good a cop to do that." The officer looked around, heading back towards the street. He lifted a hand to shade his eyes before he gave a shout and was running down the street

Bill took off after him, a sinking in his heart as he recognize a patrol vehicle. Why was it there, he asked himself. He held the door open as the patrol officer felt for a pulse, shaking his head in the negative. Bill's open hand slapped at the hood of the car. This was a good officer taken down and killed by who knows who. Whoever it was had moved the car as well.

Heading back for Sorley's, Bill called in the teams to search the area. He walked up to the front door, tapping at it lightly. Silver stood and watched him, seeing the hurt on his face that he couldn't hide.

"Bill?" Her voice caught at his attention.

"Inside, Silver. I need you to stay inside. And I need to look at your security feed."

"Where's the officer?" Silver's face paled as she realized the truth. "When?"

"Sometime overnight. The car was moved down the street. I want this person. He was too good an officer to have this happen to him."

Sorley stood behind Silver, his hands on her shoulders.

"Bill?"

"The patrol officer was killed, Sorley. We need to look at the security feeds." Silver was away, pulling up the program. "What time do you think, Bill?"

"I have no idea. Start from midnight on and go forward." Bill watched intently, see the dark form that snuck up to the patrol car just after two in the morning. He watched as well as the patrol car was moved and then the officer moved. The two figures faded around the house before a woman appeared, her face turned up to the camera as if she was boasting that she was there.

"There. She's bold, isn't she?" Silver reached to print off the photos that Bill asked for and then copied the video feed to email him.

"She's is all that, Silver. Sorley, do you recognize her?" Bill turned to find Sorley staring at the screen.

"I do, Bill. I can also tell you that she has approached me about coming in as a partner. She tried to do it through a third party but he gave up her name. That was just done or I would have told you before. I refused, not needing a partner. Even if I did, I would never go that route. Is this enough to finish this all off?"

"It is getting here. We will need to find her and bring her in. She is about the last one to arrest."

"That's why she showed up last night. If she had been able to get in, we would have ended up dead." Silver paled, feeling Sorley's hands on her shoulders.

"I need you two to stay inside. No arguments. Richard will be here shortly with the rest of your team. I have two patrol cars that will be sitting outside your door and an officer at the back door. You won't survive if you don't." Bill walked away, angry that once more his friends were at risk.

Silver turned to stare up at Sorley, finding him staring at the woman's face.

"She has family here, Silver. How do we know that they aren't involved?"

"We don't know that, Sorley. You know from your own work that we have to prove that. And that proof to be found is in Bill's hands. I just want this over." She was on her feet, wrapped in his arms, grumbling as the doorbell rang.

Chapter 43

Two days later, Bill headed for Sorley's. He had good news and bad news. They had arrested all the ones that they could. The only one still missing was the leader herself. Vi Lodge had escaped the raids of her home and business. She was in hiding and where that was, no one knew for sure. He was afraid for his friends, not certain that they were safe but praying that they were.

Silver had turned from the front door that afternoon. She had been out on the front porch, seeing that the officers had left. She had breathed a sigh of relief, thinking that it was all over with. She neglected to lock the door, thinking of something else as she walked away.

Sorley lifted his head from his work, a smile on his face. He could hear Silver singing the hymns of praise that she favoured. She was feeling as if it was all over. He agreed. His own praise raised to God, thankful that He had protected them.

An hour later, Sorley was on his feet, heading for Silver. He had her a cry from her that spurred him to almost run for her. He slid to a halt, his hands rising in the air as a weapon was pointed at him. He looked for Silver, not seeing her.

"Where is she?" When no one answered, he asked again, anger in his voice. "Where is she? What did you do with her?" He turned as he heard a sound behind him.

Silver stood there, a weapon at her temple. She was angry, he could tell, and looking for a way to escape. She stared at him, confidence in her eyes as he looked back at her.

"Well, now. We have both of you here." Vi Logan tottered into the house on her high spiked heels, barely able to stand. Her words were slurred. Neither Silver nor Sorley could tell if it was from alcohol or drugs. "We'll solve this now. You two won't see the light of another day."

Silver stood, her hands clenched, unable to move for the moment. She would wait for an opportunity. Sorley gave a slight nod, knowing that Silver would make a move when she felt it safe. He was ready to help her in any way he could, even if it meant his death.

Vi Logan paced through the house, sneering at it. It was cheap, she announced, and should just be burnt down. She returned to them, staring at first one and then the other. Her body was swaying more and more as the effects of whatever it was that she had chosen took affect. The men with her exchanged glances, knowing that she would soon be unable to give any orders. And she had not told them what she wanted them to do with the two in front of them.

No one heard the soft footfalls as men and women approached both the front of the house and then the back of it. Bill stepped inside, quiet on his feet, his weapon held in both hands. Lily followed, hearing the back door open slowly and softly and officers approaching that way.

Silver's ears had caught the sound and she breathed a sigh of relief. Help was here. Now, they just had to survive. There was no guarantee that they would.

Bill's weapon dug into the flesh just behind the man's ear even as his other hand reached for the man's weapon. Lily moved towards Vi as Jason appeared behind the man holding Sorley in stillness. Vi screamed in anger as she saw her plans going down the drain. She tried to run, a heel breaking from her left shoe.

Bill watched as the three were handcuffed and then led from the house. Silver stared at him and then at Sorley before she launched herself at him just as he moved her way. He caught her to himself as tightly as she could. Their tears mingled on their cheeks. Bill and Lily turned away, knowing that they needed a few moments.

Twenty minutes later, Bill and Lily walked back into the house. Sid and his team were working through what they needed to in collecting the evidence that was there. Sid pointed towards the office and Bill nodded as he headed that way. He stood, watching as Silver huddled in her chair and Sorley paced.

Silver's head raised as she frowned at Bill.

"Is this it, Bill? Is this over with?" Silver was hopeful but not sure that it was.

"It is, Silver. She was the last one who we needed to find. She's been in hiding for the last couple of days or it would not have come to this. She has a lot to answer for." Bill perched on a corner of the desk as Lily found a chair. "Talk to us, Silver. Sorley. I know that you have given your statements. I just want to hear what happened from you both."

Silver and Sorley looked at each other and nodded. They both talked, giving what they could. Richard and his team appeared as they finished, watching Silver closely. Richard nodded. Silver was safe and unharmed for the most part. He would find someone whom she could talk with and do the same for Sorley. They would need it, he knew.

Silver looked up at Richard, finding his smile at her helping her to calm down. Richard had a sense of peace around him all the time that she sometimes envied. She knew that it came from his walk with their God.

Bill walked away at last, promising to meet with them in a few days just to give them closure on the investigation or as much of it as he could.

Silver was on her feet, hugging her team mates, finding Sorley right behind her.

"It's over, Richard. Other than for court. Bill has them all." Silver could find the relief flowing through her. She was tired but not ready to sleep.

"That's wonderful, Silver." Richard grinned at her. "That means we need to celebrate."

"We do." Timothy grinned at her as well. "How be we have a party here on Saturday?"

"Inviting yourself, Timothy?" Sorley grinned back at him. "I think that's a wonderful idea. Anyone who has been involved in this is included."

———

Richard and the team left at last, walking away knowing that Silver and Sorley were safe. They were happy with one another, having found their life mates. He paused for a moment, eyeing the sky, a thank you lifted to the heavens.

Chapter 44

Saturday found the group gathering at Silver and Sorley's, laughter and joy spreading inside and outside of the house. Silver was glowing, happy in her life. Sorley stood and watched her, Sean and Seamus on either side of him.

"She's happy, Sorley. Thank you for being you." Seamus clapped a hand to his brother-in-law's shoulder before he walked away.

Richard took his spot, sharing a glance with Sean.

"Sorley? You're okay now?" Richard had been concerned about him.

"I am, now that this is over. I have a bride who I love and adore, family and friends that I would not trade, and a God who is faithful in all this. He has never left us. He has protected us in all things."

Bill walked through the group, looking for Silver. He found her holding his son, Michael with his arms wrapped around her neck. He grinned at his father before struggling to get down and running to find someone else to hold him.

"Silver? How are you?" Bill's question had her turning to him.

"I'm okay, Bill. I've worked through what I need to. Now, you're to update us."

"And I will. Is now a good time?"

"Yesterday was a good time. So yes." She stalked off, leaving him laughing.

Bill searched the group gathering around him. He could tell some things. Other things had to stay unspoken as they were part of the investigation and charges and would only come out in court.

"Silas? Pray for us please?"

Silas nodded, leading off a time of prayer that was quickly picked up by others in the group. A sense of peace and awe flowed through the group as they felt as if they had entered heaven.

Bill searched for Silver, finding her standing with Sorley's arms wrapped around her. He smiled to himself. Silver had always said that she would never marry. Here she was married and happy. She was glowing, he decided, making her more beautiful than she had been.

"So you want an update. Okay, this is what we can tell you. Vi Logan is all and more than what we thought. She has been deep in the crime scene here in Elmton for years. She ran some of the drug gangs. She also was involved in break and enters, using drugs as an incentive for the youth to steal and then bring her the items. They were not just simple things. She had insurance agents working for her, giving her tips as to where expensive items could be found. Jewelry, small pieces of artwork, that kind of stuff. She would then sell it on the black market here or outside the country. She was also involved in the smuggling of designer drugs. It was one of those drugs that they used on you,

Silver. She had planned that it would kill you. Only it didn't. God had His hand on you.

"She wanted it all. Her family left her and she resented that. She blamed everyone around her for her marriage failure. We have spoken with her former husband and her children.

"I think that's about all. She seemed to fixate on you two because of who you are. She's watched you two over the years, resentful that you succeeded and that you pleased your families with your lives. She decided that you would need to pay and that your families needed to pay for that. It just doesn't make sense."

"When minds turn like that, it doesn't make sense." Andrew spoke up. "We've seen it too many times. Silver. Sorley. We are thankful that you are both here and relatively unharmed. We have resources for you if you need them."

Sorley nodded. Silver and he had made arrangements for counselling and were committed to that.

"We're good, Andrew. Thank you, all of you for standing by us and getting us through this. God has blessed us with you."

Richard was the last one to walk away. He hugged Silver and then Sorley before he spoke.

"Take some time, Silver. We're all off the next week. If you need more time, let me know. When we go back to work, we'll be training. We're all set up to do that. Thanks to everyone who has pitched in to help."

Silver locked the door behind him, turning to find Sorley waiting for her. She walked into his arms, holding on, reaching for his kiss. They were now free of whatever it was that had stalked them. Silver still had a feeling that someone was after Richard, that there were unanswered questions yet to be answered. The question of the arson fire that destroyed the garage had not been explained. Vi Logan had denied any connection to it.

Sorley's hand reached for Silver's a few months later. They had snuck away for a weekend up north, finding an isolated cabin that they could use for a few days. Silver was happy, he knew, happy with the work that Richard had for her. Sorley was happy, his own work in investigations opening up more and more. He was able to pick and choose what he was wanting to do. That had changed the focus of what he did.

They were walking the streets of a small village, delighted with the shops. Silver had dragged Sorley in and out of them, their purchases growing. He had finally stopped her, kissed her, and then headed for the car, locking the bags in the trunk. He ran back towards her, delighted that he had someone to share his life.

Silver then turned to a nearby street vendor, her questions bringing a smile to the man's face. Sorley watched, seeing in her the delight and interest that she had in people. He decided that was what made her so good at her work.

He took the bag of food, leaving her to carry their drinks. Finding a bench near a river, Silver sat, watching as Sorley sat beside her. His hand reached for hers as he asked a blessing on their food.

Their meal finished, they simply sat, Sorley's arm around her holding her close to him. They had not talked through what had happened, neither one wanting to do that. They knew that they had to at some point.

"Silver, do you have any regrets?" Sorley watched her beloved face.

"Regrets? I suppose I do. We all do. I just wish that I had been a better witness for God through it all. I did grow angry and had to repent of that."

"We all grow angry at some point. God understands that. I wish that we had not had to go through what we did. I don't know that we would have become a couple if we hadn't though."

"I often ask myself that, my love. God would have brought us together. It was hard what we went through. I was so scared when you were stabbed. I was sure that I would lose you."

"It was scary. I was so afraid that something would happen to you and I would lose the love of my life. God has been gracious and faithful." Sorley grew quiet, knowing that words were not necessary.

Silver was content as well just to sit. They had talked a lot between them, getting to know one another. She knew that Sorley regretted not courting her before they married but she had reassured them that she understood.

"Sorley, what happens now?"

"Now? We go on with the life that God has granted us. We spend time with our families and friends. If God grants our desire for a family of our own, then we reassess what we do. I know that you can continue working. Richard has reassured us of that."

"I know. I just feel as if we should be doing something more. I talked to one of the support animal groups. They are looking for foster families for their puppies. That is something I have always wanted to do, but we need to be agreed on that."

"We'll pray about it, sweetheart. If it is something that you feel strongly about, we'll do it. Never fear that I will not back you on your decisions." He dropped a kiss on her temple before they both grew quiet again, contemplating their life, their love, and their heavenly Father.

They rose at last, heading for their car, intent of returning to the cabin. They were heading back to their home in Elmton the next day, back to their work. Their families were planning a party for them, to help celebrate that they were free of the danger that they had faced.

Sean and Seamus had approached them just before they had gone on their trip. The brothers had looked at one another and then at Silver and Sorley. They had asked what they could to help them recover. Silver and Sorley had looked at one another and shrugged, not sure what to say.

Sean had grinned, holding up a rake.

"We need to redo your backyard. Will you let us work on that while you are away?"

Silver had laughed and then hugged him.

"Of course, we will. Just don't go overboard."

Silver and Sorley stood the next day, staring at their yard, not recognizing it. It had been transformed into what they had envisioned between themselves.

"How did they do that?" Sorley walked the yard on the new pathway that ran the perimeter, along the new flower beds. The flower beds were filled with perennials and shrubs, just as they had talked about.

Silver had laughed, hugging him, and then walking towards the small gazebo. It had always been a dream of her to have that but she had never thought that she would. *God, this is You. You have taken our dreams and brought them to life. How we praise You for Your love and care for us. We fail you, walk away, but You are faithful and just welcome us back to You.*

Thank you for choosing to read the story of Silver and her knight, Sorley. Once again, they have taken off with the story, taking the author along for the ride. Not that I mind. They always have better plot ideas than I do.

Throughout it all, they were confident in God. His faithfulness never fails and never falls short of what we need. He knows our life story from before we were even born. He knows what we will face and how we will face it. God provides for our needs. We need never fear that He will walk away from us. We walk away from Him but He is always standing there, waiting for us.

Now as to who all has appeared in the story. Abe and Emma and his team always seem to show up. They are beloved characters whose stories are found in the *His Guardians* series. Doug and Darci's story is found in *The Heart of a Lion*. Dave and Rylee's story is *A Touch of His Garment*. Grady and Eineen's story is *Echoes of His Mercies*. Andrew and Phoebe's story is *The Potter's Hands*. Samuel and that group of friends have their stories in the series, *His Warriors*.

Richard and his team were not to have their stories told. However, they refused to let me walk away from them. They insisted that someone out there needs to read their stories. How can I dispute that? I just follow where my characters lead.

As you walk through life, never doubt that God is with You. It may be in the small things or it may be in the big things. He delights in us and in providing for us.

God bless each one of you.

Ronna

Website: ronnabacon.com